SHOOT TO KILL

SHOOT TO KILL

The Texas Rangers sent Carter O'Brien south of the border with orders to kill a madman. It was said that his target – a murderous bandit named Salazar – had the face of an angel and the heart of a demon. Given the choice, he'd sooner have faced Salazar in a head-on gunfight than turn back-shooter and kill him from hiding, but the only trouble with that idea lay with Salazar's eight-strong gang of cut-throats. It was common knowledge that if you took on one of them, you took on the lot – and even a professional fighting man like O'Brien had to draw the line somewhere...

SHOOT TO KILL

by

Ben Bridges

Dales Large Print Books
Long Preston, North Yorkshire,
BD23 4ND, England.

British Library Cataloguing in Publication Data.

Bridges, Ben
      Shoot to kill.

KENT ARTS & LIBRARIES

A catalogue record of this book is
available from the British Library

ISBN   978-1-84262-781-5 pbk

First published in Great Britain in 1990 by Robert Hale Limited

Cover illustration © Gordon Crabb by arrangement with
Alison Eldred

Published in Large Print 2010 by arrangement with
David Whitehead

Dales Large Print is an imprint of Library Magna Books Ltd.

Printed and bound in Great Britain by
T.J. (International) Ltd., Cornwall, PL28 8RW

This one is for
Guy N. Smith
– whose own books are *always*
pincer-clicking good!

ONE

'Well?' the *rurale* major asked brusquely. 'Will he live?'

The *curandero*, a bent-backed old medico whose name was Ramirez, nodded. '*Si*. But it is a miracle, Major Iniestra. He was beaten very badly. When your men brought him in here last night I did not think he would see another dawn.'

'He was that bad?'

'*Si, jefe.*'

'And now?' The major brushed dust from the sleeves of his drab olive uniform. 'What is the extent of his injuries now that you've had more time to examine him?'

'No broken bones,' Ramirez replied quickly, 'though there is much bruising of the abdomen, shoulders, lower back and face. There may be some internal damage, too, but at this stage I really could not say for sure. Still, from the look of his knuckles, I would say he gave his attackers almost as good as he got.'

With curiosity filling his smooth, tanned

face, Major Iniestra peered down at the man on the pallet beneath small, sun-filled window. Outside, life in Piedras Negras went on much as usual. The officer, a tall, well-proportioned forty-year-old, said, 'He has a name, this *Yanqui?*'

The older man nodded.

'*Si.* I went through his possessions, as Sergeant Mata instructed, and found this.'

Iniestra took a creased United States voter's card from the doctor and read the name on it thoughtfully. 'Carter O'Brien.'

'You have heard of him, *jefe?*'

'No. But the name...' Again Iniestra ran his black eyes over the sleeping man. This O'Brien was a tall *hombre*, he thought, about six feet two, and somewhere around a hundred and seventy pounds. The *rurale* major studied his tanned, battered face critically, searching for something that might help bring his hazy memory into sharper focus, but nothing about the close-cut salt-and-pepper hair, the wind-burnt face, straight nose, wide mouth or firm jaw struck him as being familiar.

Beside him, Ramirez bent forward and peeled back the sleeping man's eyelids one at a time. The orbs beneath were glazed and unseeing, a calm, transparent blue. After a brief examination, the *curandero* straightened back to his full five feet six.

'Was this all you found?' Iniestra asked, holding up the voter's card.

'No, *jefe*. There was also a fine Hunter watch. His billfold, too.'

'Hmmm. The billfold, it was empty?'

'No, Major. It contained more than one hundred American dollars.'

Iniestra puzzled over that. 'The motive wasn't robbery, then,' he mused aloud.

'Not robbery, no.'

The *rurale* cast the doctor a shrewd glance. 'What does that mean? Sounds to me as if you know more than you're letting on.'

Ramirez shrugged uncomfortably. 'It's only gossip, *jefe*. But they say he came to town yesterday afternoon, and that last night he toured the cantinas and brothels asking after ... after the Angel.'

Iniestra's eyes narrowed to slits. 'The Angel! I wonder what business this *norteamericano* had with that insurrectionist fiend?'

'I could not say, *jefe*.'

It was Major Iniestra's turn to lean over the unconscious figure. The American slept on peacefully, parting his lips every so often

11

to murmur something unintelligible.

'Who are you, *Señor* O'Brien?' Iniestra asked softly. 'What brings you here? I know your name, but I just can't place it – yet.' Abruptly he pushed himself away from the pallet and turned to face the hunched little doctor. 'I'll be assigning a man to keep watch on this fellow,' he decided. 'And I'll want you to come and fetch me the *instant* he regains his senses.'

'*Si, jefe.* It will be done.'

'If it *was* the Angel who brought this man to Piedras Negras, I want to know the connection between them. And I *will* know it, Ramirez. I *will* know.'

'I'll come straight to the point, O'Brien,' the Texas Ranger captain had said three days earlier. 'You've got quite a reputation. As a fighting-man, it seems you have few equals. And that's just what we need right now. A first-class fighting-man.'

The Texas Ranger captain sat back in his cane-bottom chair and steepled his fingers. His name was Daniel Taylor and he was forty-seven years of age. Thick, neatly-combed hair, prematurely grey at the temples, black elsewhere, was swept back from his tanned, unsmiling face. He had bushy brows, cynical blue eyes, a large, hooked nose and distaste plain on his narrow lips. He didn't like O'Brien. He didn't like anyone who took the law into his own hands by hiring out his gun. And he certainly didn't like the idea of bringing in a civilian to settle what was, essentially, a Ranger problem.

At the moment, however, he didn't have a whole lot of choice.

Sitting across the desk from him, Carter O'Brien held his silence. The blue-eyed soldier of fortune, freshly returned to more familiar climes after a blood-spattered couple of months up in Alaska, allowed his gaze to shift slightly, so that he was looking over the captain's left shoulder and out into the Ranger barracks beyond the small tar-paper window. A couple of tired, dusty men with stars on their chests, just back from patrol, stood talking in the shade out there, while a third led his droop-headed chestnut mare slowly across the parade-ground toward the stables. Above them all, a hot Texas sun beat down on the lush green land just west of Del Rio.

'Go on,' O'Brien said at last.

The captain stood up and turned around, so that he, too, could stare out through the window. He stayed like that, with his back to his guest, as he said, 'For about eight or ten months now, we've been having trouble with a gang of Spanish and American low-lives who've been raising holy Ned down along the border. We suspect their involvement in two bank robberies, a rape, a couple incidents of cattle rustling, a stagecoach hold-up and at least six murders. Whenever we've made any moves to arrest them, however—'

'—they've hightailed it across the Rio Grande into Mexico,' O'Brien guessed.

Taylor turned back to him, ran his cynical eyes across O'Brien's rugged face and nodded. 'Uh-huh. And whenever the *federales,* or Gonzalez' raggle-tail *Guardia Nacional*'ve tried to collar 'em for crimes committed in Mexico, they've done exactly the opposite.'

The Ranger captain stepped out from behind his desk and moved over to the map on the far wall. His bootfalls sounded loud in the confines of the office, and hollow, like dirt falling on a coffin lid.

'When all this began,' he said, 'the gang seemed content enough to concentrate its skulduggery in this area here, around Ciudad Acuna. In the last six months, however,

14

they've started swinging a wider loop. Their field of operations now takes in this whole two-hundred-mile stretch of border country, from Langtry in the northwest, right on down through Eagle Pass to Laredo.'

'That's a pretty wide stomping-ground,' O'Brien allowed.

'*Too* wide,' Taylor agreed, returning to the desk. 'And it's become too big a problem to ignore,' he continued bluntly. 'Folks on both sides of the Rio have started living in fear of these firebrands, O'Brien – and with good reason. They're entitled to protection, but we just haven't been able to give it. According to the Mexican authorities, these owlhoots are *our* problem. As far as the Governor of Texas is concerned it's about time the *federales* started pulling *their* weight.'

'And while the powers-that-be argue the responsibility of it,' said O'Brien, 'this gang of cut-throats keeps on killing.'

'Exactly,' Taylor responded. '*Something's* got to be done; that much is obvious. But since the Mexicans won't grant us permission to operate on their side of the border, and we won't allow them to work over *here*, just how are we supposed to handle it?'

O'Brien's smile was little more than a bemused twitch of his lips. 'Hire an independent gun,' he said. 'Me.'

Captain Taylor nodded and resumed his seat. 'You can see the reasoning of it, of course. You're not tied down by the rules and regulations. You can go *where* you want, *when* you want. You're responsible to no-one but yourself.'

'And if I'm caught or killed whilst I'm doing your dirty work,' O'Brien added easily, 'I'm just another *gringo* with no official ties.'

Taylor seemed pleased that he understood the situation. 'Precisely,' he said around a cool smile.

'There's just one thing I don't quite understand,' O'Brien said, crossing his legs. 'Just how am I supposed to stop this gang when the Texas Rangers, the *federales* and the *Guardia Nacional* can't even get near 'em?'

'Oh, that's simple,' Taylor replied, and O'Brien knew that it wasn't going to be simple at all. 'As far as we've been able to ascertain, the gang is about eight men strong. Half of 'em are mentioned in the bible,' he said, referring to the comprehensive list of wanted men that the Rangers updated and amended as the need arose. 'The rest we're not sure about.

'One thing we *do* know, however. That a common link unites all of them. Destroy

16

that link and they'll break up, drift apart, head for pastures new.'

O'Brien licked his lips. 'And in this case, the link is…?'

'Their leader,' said Taylor. 'Angel Salazar.'

O'Brien digested that. Then, just to be absolutely sure there was no misunderstandings, he said, 'So you want me to catch this Salazar and bring him in alone?'

'To hell with bringing him in,' Taylor replied, eyeing him steadily. 'We want him assassinated, O'Brien. Understand me? When you find him, we want you to *kill* him.'

O'Brien swallowed hard as he turned Taylor's words over in his mind. This little proposition was just about the last thing he'd expected to hear from the Texas Rangers. When Taylor's wire had caught up with him at his lodgings in Tombstone, Arizona, curiosity had made him come something like four hundreds miles to find out more about it. But now that he'd *heard* more, he wanted no part of it.

Oh, sure, it was true that he'd been a lot of things in his thirty-seven years – whorehouse bouncer, prize-fighter, Pinkerton detective and bounty-hawk. But never had he killed a man in such a cold, calculating

17

way. And neither was he certain he could do it now.

So he said, 'I'm sorry, captain, but I think you're talking to the wrong man.'

Taylor raised one eyebrow. 'Oh? And here I thought I was talking to the feller they say'll take on any dirty chore as long as the price is right.'

O'Brien allowed the implied insult to wash over him. 'In that case, I'd say you've *definitely* got the wrong man,' he said. 'Sure; I make a living with this,' he admitted, indicating the .38 calibre Colt Lightning in the plain brown leather gunbelt strapped around his lean hips. 'But I don't kill men from ambush, Taylor, no matter who they are, or how much they deserve to die.'

Taylor met his gaze and nodded again. 'All right,' he said. 'That's fair enough. And for what it's worth, I don't like this business any more than you do. But just try taking Salazar out in a head-to-head and see how far *that* gets you.'

O'Brien rose to his feet and clapped his tobacco-coloured Stetson firmly down on his head. 'Thanks for the offer, but I think I'll pass.'

'Just hold on a minute, O'Brien. We called you all the way down here to make you a proposition. At least hear it out.'

The freelance fighting-man hesitated, then said, 'All right; I'm listening.'

Taylor weighed something up in his mind, finally muttered, 'Come with me,' and headed for the door.

O'Brien caught up with him and together they strode along a dim, narrow corridor with white-painted adobe walls and out onto the parade-ground. The Ranger barracks had been constructed on similar lines to an Army outpost. There was a long, low barrack-room, a bath-house, mess-hall and tack shop. A few neat little stucco dwellings for Rangers with dependents ran in a line just behind the stable and corral, fairly glowing in the hard afternoon sunlight.

'I'll be honest with you, O'Brien,' Taylor said as they headed for the married men's quarters. 'The idea of playing bushwhacker turned my stomach, too. But when I got to thinking about it, I realized that killing Angel Salazar wasn't so much an act of murder. It's more like putting a rabid animal out of its misery.

'Salazar's a kill-crazy madman,' he continued. 'He's only twenty-five years old, but already he's got quite a reputation for cruelty. Comes from a well-heeled family of financiers down in Monterrey, so he doesn't commit these crimes of his for the money. He just does it out of some twisted need to kill and terrorize.

'Still, I don't expect you to take *my* word for it,' the captain remarked as they approached the last little house in the line. Reaching up, Taylor rapped on the door, then folded his arms across his star and craned his neck so that he could glance up at the azure sky.

About a quarter of a minute passed before the door opened. When it did, the two men hastily doffed their headgear, for a young girl stood there, holding the edge of the door with both hands.

She was perhaps eighteen, no older, and undoubtedly Mexican. Shoulder-length, raven-black hair framed a dark face with wide hazel eyes, a pert little nose and bold, womanly lips. Her trim figure was encased in a maroon velveteen dress, buttoned to the throat. It hugged her high breasts, encircled her narrow waist and flared out from her shapely hips to end in a soft spill at her ankles.

For just a moment her eyes lingered inquisitively on O'Brien's knocked-about face, tracing the odd, dark scars left over from his weeks spent battling with the sub-zero elements up in Alaska. Then she switched her attention to Taylor and inclined her head respectfully. *'Buenas dias, el capitan.* Please ... come inside.'

Taylor led the way and O'Brien followed, hat in hand. They stepped out of the sun and into a small living-area with a plain earth floor and a low ceiling. A Rochester lamp hung from the central beam. After dark it would glow down on an empty fireplace, an old oval mat, two frail-looking chairs and a table. O'Brien saw two doors in the facing wall. Beyond one lay a compact, functional kitchen. The other doubtless housed a bedroom.

'Senorita Rosalia,' Taylor said politely. 'May I present the man we spoke of last week – Carter O'Brien.'

'Senor,' she said quietly.

O'Brien nodded.

'Is your pappy around...?' asked Taylor.

'I am here.'

They all swung to face the direction from which the new voice had come. The bedroom door had clicked open and a seventy-year-old Mexican sitting in a green-enamelled wheelchair with a high, uncomfortable-looking back shoved himself forward. He looked

21

much older than his years, with white hair, a drooping moustache and oh-so-tired eyes of some dark, indeterminate colour, and his expensive grey suit hung loosely on his sadly-emaciated form.

He continued pushing at the squeaking wheels to either side of his chair, obviously finding it hard work, but not once did his daughter offer assistance. Maybe she knew better than to undermine what was left of his pride.

Finally he reached them, then shook their hands with typical Mexican formality. His grip, O'Brien noticed, was weak, and one side of his face bore a slack, lifeless look that hinted at a recent stroke.

'*Buenas dias,*' he said to Taylor.

The Texas Ranger again introduced O'Brien, and the old man told them to sit down. When they were comfortable, Taylor explained to O'Brien, '*Senor* Laurencio's been staying here as our, ah, guest, for the last three weeks.'

'And you're connected in some way to this business with Angel Salazar,' O'Brien prodded, eyeing the old man.

Senor Laurencio inclined his head. 'Indeed I am,' he replied in a once-strong voice that now seemed weak and phlegmy. 'For it was

Angel who put me into this wheelchair. Angel who took his gun and deliberately shattered my legs at the knees. Angel who turned me into the pitiful creature you see before you now.'

There wasn't really much O'Brien figured he could say to that, so he said nothing.

'I don't know how much the *capitan* has told you about Angel...?' the old man asked expectantly.

'Only that he's a half-crazy maniac who kills for sport.'

Senor Laurencio nodded sadly. 'Well, that is true enough, saints help us. Angel! What a name for a boy who acts more like the devil! But he was not always like that, *senor.* There was a time when all the innocence of the world could be found in his face. A beautiful child, he was. Beautiful.

'But a few months after his seventeenth birthday, something evil entered into him and took possession of his soul. A demon, perhaps? I do not know. He was hardly the same boy after that, though. He had only to see a cat lazing in the shade and he could barely resist the urge to kick it. In his eyes, a bird crossing the sky ahead of him existed only as some kind of target by which he could prove his marksmanship. A wicked boy, he became,' lamented the old Mexican. 'Wicked, and sick in the head.'

Tears glistened in his dull, lifeless eyes, and made them sparkle for an instant, until he palmed them away with rough, angry movements.

'Papa–' said the girl with concern.

Ignoring her, he again concentrated his attention on O'Brien. 'It was not a pretty thing to see, *senor*. Corruption is never pretty. And what it did to Angel was almost too hideous to behold, for it turned him into something ugly and unclean; a fiend masquerading as a man.

'We at the *Hacienda* Salazar did what we could to curb his vile and violent nature, but it was not easy, and no remedy lasted long. Right up until that final night when all of his evil came boiling to the surface and he raped his own sister and crippled me, we had hoped that he would change ... grow out of his wicked ways...'

Again tears flooded his eyes, and this time he let them trickle sluggishly down his miserly cheeks unheeded. 'But we were wrong,' he said, 'And foolish. The evil within him was too strong to suppress.

'Angel is indeed a madman, *senor*. A madman who worships death, destruction and depravity. I realize that now. We *all* do. And that is why I beseech you to do this thing that the *capitan* asks. Kill Angel for us. End *his* suffering, *senor*. End the suffering of his family.' His lower lip trembled pitifully. 'For the love of all that is holy,' he said, 'kill my son, I beg you.'

O'Brien's mouth fell open and his eyes widened in surprise. Up till now he'd assumed the old man to be an uncle or maybe some kind of family retainer. Taylor must have seen the surprise in his face, because he said, 'Yes, O'Brien. This is *Senor* Laurencio Alejandro Govea Salazar – Angel's father.'

The old man was dying by inches, and shame was his killer.

He had lost everything because of his son – his pride, his business, his friends, the use of his legs. His wife Blanca had died about half a year earlier, of a broken heart, he said, and his standing within the community had crumbled rapidly as each new outrage of Angel's filtered down from the border country.

Now he had nothing.

But he was at pains to stress that he did not want his son murdered out of any desire

25

for revenge, however, and O'Brien, shifting his gaze from the pathetic old man to Rosalia, who was struggling hard to keep her own tears in check, believed him.

Still, could he kill a man from ambush? Back-shooting went against everything he believed in. But the more he looked at the wretched human ruin *Senor* Laurencio had become; the more he thought about the torment the old man's beautiful daughter must have suffered at the hands of her own brother; the more he heard about Angel's many perversions – *so the more O'Brien thought he might be able to do it after all.*

It turned out that *Senor* Laurencio had originally gone to seek an audience with President Gonzalez himself in order to settle this thing with Angel once and for all. But Gonzalez had other things on his mind, and one *loco* bandit riding roughshod over the border-land was the least of his worries.

So the old man had gone to the *jefe de federales,* only to find the same reluctance to interfere. It was an American problem, he was told, and the *federales* had neither the men nor the resources to cover two hundred miles of country just to find and arrest one man.

26

Senor Laurencio had come north to Austin, Texas then, and put his case to the Governor. He was tired and dying, he said. But before he went to meet his Maker, he wanted to see his only son's reign of madness ended.

The Governor had been moved by the old man's plight; mindful, too, that something must indeed be done about the fear Angel was creating along the northern banks of the Rio Grande. So he promptly sent the old man to the Texas Rangers with a recommendation that Captain Taylor find him a place to stay until the matter was resolved. It was *Senor* Laurencio himself who had come up with the idea to assassinate Angel, and while the Rangers could not officially condone or sanction his murder, they had to admit that if a man could be found who would do the deed, it would solve an awful lot of problems for all concerned.

'Well?' Rosalia asked softly when her father and the Ranger captain finished talking thirty minutes later. 'My father is prepared to pay you well for your trouble, *senor.* Will you help us?'

O'Brien held back for just a second. Then he said, 'Yes.'

The old man's shoulders slumped with relief. 'Thank God,' he husked. '*Senor,* it is

27

a great service you will perform by–'

'Forget it,' O'Brien interrupted, harder than intended. But he wasn't at all sure that he'd made the right decision. Now that he'd come right out and committed himself, the spell had been broken and he began to realize just what he was letting himself in for. Still, there was no denying that for the good of all, Angel Salazar must die. 'Captain – I'll need as much information on Angel and his gang as you can give me. *Senor* Laurencio – from you I'll need a description of your son.'

'We can do better than that,' said Rosalia, swishing over to the mantel. 'We can give you this.'

She handed O'Brien a thick, sepia-toned daguerreotype of a handsome young man in his middle-teens. His face was round and angelic, his eyes dark and well-spaced above a long nose with flared nostrils and a wide, happy mouth. The boy had a clear complexion and shining black hair slicked flat to his skull. In the picture he was wearing a form-fitting suit, the jacket cut to waist-length, the pants tight across the hips and groin. He looked to be tall and slim.

'This was taken just after Angel's sixteenth birthday,' the girl said in a curiously

28

business-like way. 'Despite the ugliness that consumed him from within, his physical appearance has not greatly changed.'

O'Brien nodded without taking his faded blue eyes from the smiling young boy in the daguerreotype. The boy in whose face could be found all the innocence of the world.

The boy he had just undertaken to kill.

TWO

O'Brien rode his feisty little quarter-horse into Piedras Negras two days later, his blue eyes moving warily beneath the shade of his hat-brim and his calico workshirt, creased brown cords and low-heeled cowman's boots yellowed from the dust of the trail.

The bustling Mexican town lay just across the Rio Grande from Eagle Pass, some sixty miles to the south and east of the Ranger barracks in Del Rio; O'Brien reached it via the bridge spanning the muddy, fast-flowing water that formed a natural border between the two countries, and angled the horse slowly in among the narrow maze of chili-scented streets.

Piedras Negras was largely unremarkable, little more than a jumble of low, sand-coloured *jacales* encircling a few cantinas, gambling-rooms, three churches, a few stores and a brothel or six. Following the dusty, crooked little alleyways toward the centre of town, where rose an ornate well and fountain and one or two municipal buildings, such as the office of the *jefe politico,* or head man, O'Brien saw a sturdy-looking jailhouse and a small headquarters building belonging to the rural police. Spying a large wooden structure with the sign CABALLERIZA over the open double doors, he headed that way, dismounted and paid a gap-toothed ten-year-old in a baggy white shirt and pants to tend to his horse. He was happy to leave his comfortable old Texas double-rig in the cool, hay-smelling shadows of the stable, but took his saddle-bags, warbag and virtually priceless Winchester 'One In One Thousand' with him when he left.

According to the information he'd been able to get from Captain Taylor, Angel Salazar and his eight-strong gang of cut-throats often used Piedras Negras as a stopping-off point between raids, Taylor believed that Angel had a sweetheart there, maybe one of the *putas* working the brothels on the edge of the commercial district. Certainly the madman had been sighted there on a number of different occasions, and apparently the local law seemed happy enough to let him come and go unchallenged.

With nothing better to work on, O'Brien had decided that the town with its reflection in the *Rio Bravo del Norte* was going to be his most promising starting-point. But his enquiries would have to be discreet, for Angel might have spies anywhere, and O'Brien had no desire to tip his hand *just* yet.

Lugging his gear over one shoulder, he set off across the wide, sun-bleached plaza in search of a hotel, dodging fat Mexican women and malnourished men going about their business around him. The time was just a little before noon and the day was hot, so O'Brien decided to find himself a bath and a change of clothes just as soon as he'd located a room.

It was in that moment that the Hotel Isabel hove into sight about midway along the north-facing block. It was a three-storey structure of whitewashed adobe, all archways and pillars, and easily the tallest building in this part of the town. O'Brien headed toward it, booked into a fairly plain room (a brass bed, a peeling wardrobe, a washstand and a ladder-back chair complete with spur-scars), then went to find a barbershop and get a bath.

Later, once *siesta*-time took hold of the town, the streets emptied out and fell silent. Even those few fellow-Americans he'd seen earlier, sampling the dubious delights of the local cantinas, were nowhere to be seen.

The afternoon passed slowly. Up in his second-floor front room, O'Brien lay on his bed and smoked a cigarette, staring up at the peeling yellow ceiling above and wondering exactly how he was going to find his target … and how, when the time came, he was going to overcome his natural reluctance to bushwhack and blow the Angel right the way to Hell.

After a time O'Brien dozed off. The next time he opened his eyes, the worst of the day's heat had passed over and the sky beyond the fly-blown window was a deep and smoky five o'clock blue.

The compact soldier of fortune swung up off the bed, doused his face with lukewarm water from the bowl on the washstand, strapped on his gunbelt and grabbed his hat. He was hungry, and still had some time to kill before beginning his tour of the cantinas and brothels. First stop some food, then. After that he'd start making enquiries.

A warm but refreshing breeze had picked up. It blew the strong river smell down the narrow streets. O'Brien paused outside the hotel, glanced right, then left, spotted a beanery further along the other side of the thoroughfare and headed for it.

Not for the first time he found himself considering the power even an invisible barrier could wield. Take Piedras Negras, for example. It was a border town, no more than an easy five-minute horse-ride from the bridge leading back to the United States. And yet the town might just as well have been located right in the very heart of Mexico for all the American influence it displayed. The only language he heard as he crossed the street was rapid-fire Spanish, and from a cantina next door to the hotel issued the sounds of a guitar and a trumpet playing pleasant, but unmistakably Latin, music for its patrons. The air itself smelled different, too, muggy beneath the breeze and full of spices.

O'Brien entered the cafe and glanced around. Trade was still relatively slow at this hour, and consisted of little more than a handful of *peones*. He found a vacant table easily enough, and quickly claimed it. About thirty seconds later a still-attractive forty-year-old with her lustrous black hair worn in a pony-tail appeared through a curtain of beads strung across the alcove to his right and sighting him, came to take his order.

Although O'Brien could speak fluent

Spanish when the occasion demanded it, he always made a point of appearing clumsy with the language around folks who could turn out to be useful sources of information to him. He tended to pick up a lot more that way than he might otherwise. So he made his request for *mole de guajolote*, tortillas and hot chocolate seem awkward and laboured, allowing the waitress to help him with the words whenever she grew tired of his verbal stumblings.

When she finally went away he sat back in his chair and surveyed the room more thoroughly. The air was thick with the smells of food and cooking, and a comfortable buzz of conversation mingled with the rattle and clink of knives and china. The lighting was poor, for the windows at the front of the place were not very large, and the majority of tables were cloaked in gloom.

His eyes stopped their roving when they lit upon a fellow-*Yanqui* chewing up a mess of fried tortilla and beans. The fellow looked big and solid, forty-five-years-old, with an oblong face and squinting eyes. His sorry-looking curl-brimmed grey hat sat at his side, and his head, bald but for a shading of stubble, shone dully in the poor light.

Meeting O'Brien's gaze, he raised one

hand to wave a greeting. As he did so, his fleshy lips arranged themselves into a smile.

O'Brien returned the salute just as the waitress brought his order. The fricassee looked good, and he set to with relish, washing down the savoury mixture of turkey, tomatoes and sesame seeds with occasional swallows of cinnamon-spiced hot chocolate.

By the time he was ready to pay the tab, the café was beginning to crowd up some, and the table at which his countryman had been sitting was now occupied by four chattering Mexicans, a father and three of his sons, judging by the resemblance between them. Back out on the street O'Brien pulled his gold Hunter from his pants-pocket and checked the time. It was a quarter to six; time to start asking around.

The story he gave to the owner of Pablo's Cantina fifteen minutes later remained much the same as the one he told to just about every other dispenser of cheer working in the Piedras Negras bars that evening. After first checking out the clientele at each establishment in turn, he struck up conversations with barflies and whores alike, intimating that he had come south to escape some unspecified ruckus with the U.S. law. Only when he was certain he could take the exchange further without causing any unnecessary trouble did he make enquiries about the local peace-keepers.

Invariably, both the *jefe politico* and the town constable were painted as lazy, good-for-nothing freeloaders, out only to line their own pockets at the tax-payers' expense.

'A feller looking to keep his head low for a while wouldn't have much trouble from the town constable, then,' O'Brien prodded.

The bartender at the third cantina chuckled. 'Tha's one way to put eet, I guess.'

'That explains it, then,' O'Brien said with a knowing wink.

The bartender frowned. 'Explains wha'?'

'Why they're always seeing Angel Salazar around these parts. Hell, that's one feller I'd say could *use* a friendly lawman.'

Almost without fail, the mention of Angel's name caused the people he spoke to to clam up or change the subject. But even their obvious reluctance to discuss the outlaw proved one thing, however. Angel Salazar was definitely a regular visitor to Piedras Negras. O'Brien could hardly imagine anyone displaying so much hesitancy in talking about the man if he visited their town only rarely.

It was around ten o'clock that O'Brien

finally decided he wasn't going to get any more information tonight. He had a full bladder and an aching head, and he figured he'd come up against enough box canyons for one evening.

That was when a great big paw came down hard on his left shoulder.

Turning, he found himself, in an eyeball-match with the *Yanqui* he'd seen over at the cafe earlier on. Up close, the big man had a homely face and a guileless smile. His tobacco-stained teeth were even but his nose was lumpy and once-broken. His denim pants, red check shirt, buckskin vest and scratched .45 Colt identified him as a cowboy by trade. His accent was unmistakably Texan.

'Howdy,' he said, offering his right hand. 'The name's Shep Morgan. Buy you a drink?'

O'Brien glanced up at the big man and guessed his height at somewhere around six feet six. He looked Shep Morgan right in the face but found nothing there except a genuine desire to be neighbourly.

Deciding it would be impolite to refuse, then, he nodded. 'Sure. Much obliged.' He introduced himself, they shook and Morgan leaned forward to order two *cervezas*.

When the beers arrived, the bigger man

suggested they find a table, and slowly they made a circuit of the crowded cantina, past a two-piece band playing a catchy little tune and a couple of dancing-girls whirling in ever-faster circles to the encouragement of their clapping and whistling audience.

As the two men sampled the flat *cerveza*, they watched the girls appreciatively. The more they twirled, the wider the girls' skirts fanned out, revealing neatly-turned ankles.

Shep Morgan, it turned out, worked on a cattle-spread just outside Crystal City. He'd just come back from a trail-drive up to Fort Worth, and with money in their pockets, he and a few friends had decided to ride south for a week's-worth of hoot'n' holler.

Shep, however, was older than his companions, and somewhat shy around women. 'Even the kind you pay fer,' he added ruefully. So he'd left them to it, figuring to spend the evening alone.

'What is it brings *you* to these parts?' he asked at length.

'Work,' O'Brien replied vaguely. As the girls finished their act, he took the opportunity of joining in the general applause to change the subject.

Morgan, however, wasn't going to be put off. 'This work,' he said carefully. 'Wouldn't have nothin' to do with them three fellers over by the door, would it?'

The girls hurried away and the two-piece band struck up a slower, more relaxing melody. As it washed over them, O'Brien met the Texan's gaze. A moment later he moved his line of vision a little to one side, so that he could take in the trio Morgan was talking about.

All three were Mexican. The first was tall and bald, with a swarthy face and a thick black beard. He was maybe forty, slim but muscular. The man beside him was shorter, bigger of belly, about the same age but clean-shaven. His round face and hooked nose looked grey beneath the shadow of his wide sombrero. The third fellow was dark, young, so good-looking he was almost painful to behold. He was dressed entirely in black, a colour that seemed to match his smouldering eyes.

Each of them wore a gun at his belt.

'Well?' Morgan asked.

'Nothing to do with me,' O'Brien replied, betraying none of the disquiet now stirring sluggishly in his guts. 'Why should they be?'

''Cause they've been followin' you ever since you quit Pablo's place 'round six-thirty,' Morgan told him. 'That's why.'

40

O'Brien renewed his scrutiny of the Texan. Morgan read the question in his face and his disarming smile broadened slowly. 'Don't fret, cousin. I'm on your side. Saw you leavin' Pablo's myself, then spied them fellers lightin' out after you. Got curious, I guess. Nothin' better to do all by my lonesome, so *I* lit out after *them.*' He sobered abruptly. 'They're doggin' you all right, mister, an' I figured you ought to know about it.'

'Obliged.' O'Brien took another pull at his beer, eyeing his three shadows once again.

Who were they? Common thieves, out to roll a rich, drunken *gringo?* Or friends of the Angel, alerted to O'Brien's presence by all the questions he'd been asking?

'Be glad to keep you comp'ny fer the rest o' the evenin',' Morgan offered gently, breaking through his line of speculation. 'Iffen you'd like. I can be a powerful dissuader when I put my mind to it.'

O'Brien forced a smile and set his empty schooner down. 'I'll just bet you can,' he said, keeping his tone light. 'And I appreciate the offer. But there's no need.'

'I ain't so sure. They look a right mean crew to me.'

Silently O'Brien had to agree. But if they *were* somehow connected to Angel, he didn't

41

want to scare them off. They might be the best – not to mention *only* – lead he was going to get in Piedras Negras.

'Forget it,' O'Brien said, rising to his feet. 'But happen you're still around tomorrow, it'll be my turn to buy the drinks. Deal?'

'Happen *you're* still around,' Morgan said seriously. 'I'll be happy to accept.'

O'Brien reached down and they shook hands once again. Then he edged through the crowd, right past the grim-looking trio and went outside.

The air had cooled off considerably. Now it was downright pleasant. Save for the muted sounds of merriment coming from the scattered cantinas, gambling-rooms and brothels, the near-empty street was quiet. In the distance a dog howled mournfully at the full moon, but that was all.

O'Brien turned left and headed back the way he'd come, towards his hotel. Behind him, the cantina door swung open again and an oblong of hazy light fell out onto the dusty earth.

Three silhouettes stepped into the street.

O'Brien heard them, but kept walking at a steady pace, his manner giving no hint of the tension coiling his muscles ever more tight.

Three to one, he thought. Dismal odds, all right. But what the hell? A lead was a lead, wasn't it? Coolly he decided that he would take out the big feller first, then the kid. As the least-threatening member of the trio, the sombrero-wearing lard-belly could wait till last.

He strode on.

Or rather, *tried* to.

Before he could take another pace, however, something long, thin and rough suddenly cut into his calves, encircled his legs and pinned them together. With an involuntary grunt of surprise, he stumbled forward, off-balance.

Even as he slammed to the ground, he cursed himself for a fool. He'd expected them to wait till he reached the shadow-filled alleyway directly ahead before making their move. He'd banked on hearing their approach, too.

The one thing he hadn't allowed for was the chance that one of them might be carrying a *bolas*.

South American Indians had been among the first to use the weapon – in this case, a three-foot length of hemp weighted at either end with a four-pound lead ball. They flung it in such a way that it wrapped itself around the legs of fleeing animals and trapped them where they were.

The three Mexicans now racing towards O'Brien were using it for approximately the same purpose.

Before the freelance fighting-man could loosen the rope around his legs, they were upon him. One of them kicked him in the back and instinctively he curled himself into a ball. He felt another boot, this time in the ribs; a third and a fourth. Then rough hands fastened around his arms and yanked him erect.

The *bolas* was removed from his legs, but before O'Brien could do anything about regaining his balance, someone – Lard-Belly, he thought – punched him in the stomach.

While he was still bent forward, the kid and the big bald fellow with the beard hauled him toward the alleyway. Dimly O'Brien knew that once they got him in the shadows he was finished. Desperately he began to drag his feet to gain a few precious moments in which to shake the stars from his eyes. But Baldy and the kid weren't having any of it.

Baldy growled something he didn't quite catch and increased his grip on O'Brien's left arm. After that he felt himself propelled forward even faster. Behind him, Lard-Belly tucked the *bolas* into his belt and trotted along in their wake.

The shadows of the alleyway ate them up.

O'Brien was shoved against a wall. He felt the rough, cold adobe through his shirt. One of the Mexicans punched him in the stomach again and he fell forward with a groan. Finding his pain amusing, Lard-Belly laughed softly.

He was still laughing when O'Brien, now down on his haunches, suddenly lashed out with a punch of his own.

The kid was nearest, so he got it first. Without mercy, O'Brien slammed straight up into his crotch, and the kid let go a high, womanish screech and stumbled backwards, cradling his eggs. Beside him, Baldy made a sound of surprise. Within an instant, however, O'Brien was up and on him, knowing that he had to forget his own pain for the moment, and concentrate on overcoming his would-be assailants before they could inflict some more.

He was all over the big bald man, his lefts, rights, jabs and crosses honed to perfection by his time spent prize-fighting years before.

But this wasn't a boxing-match. And while the kid might not be in any fit state to cause him more grief for a while, there was still

45

Lard-Belly to contend with.

O'Brien ducked under Baldy's clumsy roundhouse right and let him have a drum-roll on the ribs. Then he spun to face the sombrero-wearing roughneck just as Lard-Belly came at him with something that looked very much like a machete in his right fist.

O'Brien dodged to one side just as the thick blade whistled overhead and clanged against the adobe wall. A stray shaft of moonlight fell off the machete as Lard-Belly swung it in another arc.

O'Brien stepped back a pace, almost fell over the kid, who was crouching now, and moaning at the ache in his groin. Righting himself, he took another pace away from the scything machete—

—straight into Baldy's waiting arms.

As the big man's fingers locked around his biceps, O'Brien immediately fought to break the hold, again cursing himself for a fool. Behind him, Baldy hissed, 'Quick, Emilio – in the stomach!' and Lard Belly – Emilio – stabbed forward with the blade.

Teeth clenched fit to shatter, O'Brien braced himself for the killing cut, still struggling to break Baldy's hold even though the bigger man's grip was vice-like.

But before the machete could do its work, it became Lard-Belly's turn to stumble over the kid crouching in the shadows.

Staggering, the Mexican said something vile in Spanish, kicked the kid himself, then began to claw his way back up to his feet.

By that time, however, O'Brien was making the most of his momentary reprieve.

With a roar, he forced Baldy to twist a little to the right. Then he back-pedalled for all he was worth until the big man came up hard against the adobe wall. Baldy started muttering something about the *gringo* sonofabitch holding still, but before he could finish his sentence, O'Brien jerked his head back into his captor's face.

Baldy loosened his grip at once, and O'Brien needed no second urging to pull away. Almost immediately Lard-Belly came at him again with the machete held high. O'Brien let him blunder past, like a *toreador* dodging a bull, then grabbed the arm wielding the long knife and snapped it neatly at the elbow.

But victory was to be short-lived. Even as the machete hit the dirt and Lard-Belly started howling like a *lobo,* Baldy was back, kicking, punching and gouging like a madman. O'Brien tried to fight back, but the big man's temper was up, and his attack displayed no logic.

To make matters worse, the kid was back on his feet, too, and joining in the onslaught. The pair of them were no more than shifting shadows in the darkness of the alley, but solid enough whenever their blows made contact.

A fist grazed O'Brien's brow and snapped his head sideways. He got in a lucky punch of his own, but it was destined to be his last. In the star-spattered blackness of the narrow thoroughfare, he finally had to acknowledge the pain of blow after blow, and cursing like crazy, began to sink to his knees.

Another punch; another; a kick; a knee in the chest. Suddenly, in all the chaos, his bladder relaxed. A dark stain appeared at the crotch of his pants, and that infuriated him more than anything else.

Then the beating stopped, and Baldy grabbed him awkwardly by his short salt-and-pepper hair while the kid picked up the machete and slowly drew it back in readiness for a blow that would sever his head.

O'Brien croaked, '...no...'

And somewhere a million or two miles away someone else yelled, 'Hey, there! Step aside from that feller, or so help me I'll plug you where you stand!'

Shep Morgan!

Baldy swore; O'Brien felt the fingers tangled in his hair let go. For a second or so he blacked out whilst still on his knees. Then consciousness returned and he heard all three of the Mexicans running away.

He slipped out of it again, only to pull himself stubbornly back in. By then Morgan was skidding to a halt and hunkering down beside him. 'O'Brien? O'Brien! You all right, boy? Answer me, dammit!'

But although O'Brien's mashed lips fought to reply, nothing came out save an eerie, tired moan. Then a wave of nausea flooded over him, and unable to fight it off this time, he fell forward and down … down … down into oblivion.

For a long time there was nothing; no light and no dark; no pain and no peace. O'Brien just lay corpse-still on the pallet in the small back room, his slumber deep and recuperative.

Twenty-four hours passed that way, until at last he opened his eyes once more.

The room was bright with late-afternoon sunlight. The walls were white, the floor swept earth covered with a round, claret-coloured mat. There was an old chest of drawers, an empty bookshelf and a chromo-lithograph of the Virgin up on the facing wall.

O'Brien wondered where the hell he was.

Carefully he checked his hands and arms. Movement was no problem, though it did start off one or two dull aches in his shoulders and chest. He peered thoughtfully at his knuckles. They were slightly puffed and discoloured.

He'd been in a fight, then.

That brought it all back to him; Angel Salazar, Shep Morgan, the fight in the alley-way.

Slowly he threw back the sheet and sat up. Someone had stripped him down to his combinations. Smelled as if they'd covered him in horse-liniment, too. Standing up awoke fresh pain, but not so much that he couldn't ignore it. He closed his eyes. Once the world stopped spinning, he was able to stamp across to the chest of drawers and start looking for his clothes.

He found everything except his bill-fold, gun and weapons-belt in the top drawer, and packing the soft pile under one arm, he grabbed his boots from beside the chest and went back to the bed to start dressing.

He was just buttoning up his stained pants when the door opened behind him. Startled, he turned fast, *too* fast, and came face to face with a short, bent-backed old Mexican of about five and sixty summers.

For a moment neither man said a word, just exchanged glances of appraisal. The old man had a shock of white hair and a wispy forked beard. His eyes were brown and fathomless. He wore a shabby black suit and an open-necked white shirt with no collar.

Finally, the old man said in passable English, 'You are awake.'

O'Brien nodded.

'How do you feel?'

'Fine.'

The old man came deeper into the room and closed the door behind him. 'Well, you don't *look* fine,' he said quietly. 'Sit down, let me see for myself.'

He was a doctor, then.

O'Brien sank down onto the mattress, glad of the opportunity to take the weight off. He'd gone without food for too long and now hunger, mingled with the punishment he'd taken in the alleyway, was making him feel a bit light-headed.

As the old man took hold of his face and tilted it up to the window, he introduced himself as Dr Carlos Ramirez. Then he told O'Brien to look straight ahead and covered his right eye with one cool, smooth palm. When he took his hand away he studied the contraction of O'Brien's pupil keenly. He repeated the action on the other eye, then covered both of them, waiting a second, then took his hands away without warning.

'I told you, doc, I'm fine,' O'Brien croaked in a voice grown used to silence.

The medico stood back. '*Si*,' he remarked. 'You are well enough, I would say.'

O'Brien frowned. 'Well enough?' he echoed. 'Well enough for what?'

'To see Major Iniestra,' said the *curandero*.

O'Brien suddenly felt a warning tingle irritate his belly. 'Who the hell's *he?*' he asked softly.

Ramirez' face aged dramatically in the late afternoon sunlight. 'A man you would be wise not to cross,' he replied, turning to head back to the door.

THREE

Closing the door quietly behind him, the doctor left O'Brien alone to ponder this new turn of events on the edge of the mattress.

Of course, the coming interview with Major Iniestra might be nothing more than a routine investigation into his beating-up. But O'Brien didn't feel too hopeful about that. He'd been asking around after the Angel. What if the *rurales* had got wind of *that?* For all they knew, O'Brien might be an owlhoot looking to join the maniac's band of killers; that was certainly the impression he himself had given during his tour of the cantinas and gambling-rooms.

Ignoring his stomach's impatient growl of hunger, he stood up, grabbed his shirt and slipped it on. He stamped into his boots next, then hustled over to the door. It might cause more problems than it would solve to light out before the major got here, but O'Brien was willing to take the chance. His palm folded around the door handle and gave it a gentle twist. The lock clicked, the door opened.

O'Brien stepped out into a narrow, white-walled passage.

'*Alto, hombre!*'

A young, acne-scarred man dressed in the ill-fitting olive uniform of the rural police had been slouching in a ladder-back chair at the far end of the passage. As soon as the bedroom door opened and O'Brien appeared, the guard had snatched up his regulation Marlin rifle and brought it to half-cock.

'*Alto!*' he barked again, standing up.

O'Brien raised his hands, having no wish to succumb to what the Mexicans called the *ley fuga,* and be shot whilst trying to escape. 'All right, all right!' He went back into the bedroom and kicked the door shut.

Flight was out of the question, then – assuming he had anything to flee *from*. He went over to the window and peered out across the plaza, enjoying the warmth of the sun on his bruised face.

Before long there was a stirring of movement over at the *rurale* headquarters on the other side of the ornate well and fountain. A door opened and Dr Ramirez came out followed by a stiff-backed officer in a peaked cap and full uniform. Watching them cross the plaza on their way back to the doctor's home, he got his first good look at Major Iniestra.

The *rurale* officer stood tall, with long arms and a confident stride. After a while he overtook Ramirez and the hunched little medico had to scurry after him like a pet dog.

Nearer they came, until O'Brien could make out the smooth, tanned face beneath the peaked cap's shadow; a face of some forty years, with black eyes and much intelligence; shrewd and wary but not at all as arrogant or unpleasant as he had expected.

O'Brien stepped away from the window and set his weight back down on the mattress. About five minutes later he heard the front door close, footsteps drum on the floor outside, the respectful *click* of the guard's heels as he snapped to attention.

A moment later the bedroom door opened, and the doctor led the officer into the room.

Keeping his eyes on O'Brien, the major swept off his cap and said, 'That will be all, thank you Ramirez. You may leave us now.'

Ramirez dipped his head eagerly. *'Si, jefe.'*

He closed the door behind him on his way out.

A quarter of a minute passed in silence. Finally the *rurale* smoothed down his oiled black hair and said, *'Buenas dias, senor.'*

O'Brien nodded. 'Howdy.'

Taking the hint, the officer switched to heavily-accented English. 'I am Major Juan Iniestra, commander of the *rurale* detachment stationed here at Piedras Negras. And it is possible that *you, Senor* O'Brien, are in very serious trouble indeed.'

O'Brien narrowed his eyes. 'Trouble? Why? For allowing myself to get beaten up?'

Iniestra didn't reply directly. Instead he fired another question. 'What brought you to Piedras Negras, *senor?*'

O'Brien shrugged. 'This and that.'

'Trouble with the American authorities, perhaps?'

'Nope.'

'Are you *sure?*'

'I'm sure.'

'You are not wanted by the law, then?'

'Not at all.'

'Then what is your connection with Angel Salazar?'

'Salazar?'

'Oh, come now, do not insult me by feigning ignorance. You spend one entire evening questioning various *paisanos* about

56

him. Who *are* you, O'Brien? What did you want with the Angel?'

O'Brien drew in a slow, stubborn breath. 'I don't know what you're talking about,' he said quietly.

Iniestra made a sound of mild irritation. 'That is a shame,' he said. 'Because to those who cooperate, I can be a forgiving man. But to those who persist in keeping secrets...' He smiled coolly. 'I'm sure you understand.'

Wandering over to the window, he peered outside. The sunlight accentuated the smoothness of his face. 'I know your name from somewhere O'Brien,' he said pleasantly. 'I just can't recall the context yet.'

'O'Brien's a common enough name.'

'Perhaps. But not here in Mexico.' He turned away from the window. 'Now, one last time; why were you so interested in the Angel? You had some business to conduct with him, maybe?'

'No business,' O'Brien replied. 'No *interest.*'

Iniestra sucked in one cheek. 'And that is your final word?'

'I don't see what else I can say.'

'Very well. You leave me no choice but to transfer you to the *calabozo* until you change your mind.'

'*Jail!* Hold on, now, major? You can't put me away; I haven't *done* anything!'

'Then let us call it protective custody,' Iniestra said smugly. He turned and went over to the door, his black, knee-high riding-boots sounding dull against the earthen floor. 'You are a fool, *senor*,' he said with mock regret. 'You know you had only to answer my questions and this entire matter would have been resolved. As it is, I now have no option but to call in the *colorados*. *They* will get some answers out of you, I'm certain.'

O'Brien felt a sudden stab of foreboding. The *colorados* were the pick of the Government's forces. Cool, cruel and ruthless, they were feared even by their opposite numbers in the *federales*. Iniestra was right, he thought. They probably *would* get some answers out of him. They'd *beat* 'em out.

'All right,' he said tightly. 'All right … the truth, then.'

Iniestra smiled. 'I'm listening.'

O'Brien hesitated for a moment, discomfort plain on his face. Then he said, 'You see that man out there, just in front of the livery stable? The one with the black hair?'

Iniestra moved away from the door, deeper into the room, sinking his head a little into his shoulders in order to stare out the window. 'Which one?' he asked.

'That one,' said O'Brien – twisting around suddenly to punch the *rurale* in the face.

The blow took Iniestra completely by surprise, and played merry hell with O'Brien's already-tender knuckles. As the major stumbled backwards, however, he followed up with a left, another right, until Iniestra came up hard against the chest of drawers, groaning.

Grabbing a fistful of the major's uniform, O'Brien raised his free hand menacingly. Iniestra didn't look so smooth now, he saw with satisfaction. The *rurale's* face was screwed up with pain; an ugly red mark was coming up on his left cheek and a thin line of blood was worming down his chin from a split lip.

'*You*–'

'Not a word, major!'

Iniestra read the threat in his eyes and shut up.

'That's better,' O'Brien said after a moment. Without taking his gaze from the other man's face, he lowered his free hand and quickly yanked Iniestra's pistol from the button-down holster at his left hip.

Just feeling the weight of the gun in his

hand made O'Brien feel better. 'Now,' he said quietly. 'Call that guard in here.'

Carefully Iniestra reached up to wipe the blood from his lip before it could drip onto his tunic. 'You're *loco*,' he said.

'*Do* it.'

'But you can't hope to get away–'

O'Brien jammed the pistol, a French-made Lefauchex revolver, right in his face. 'There's two ways to get that guard in here,' he hissed sharply. 'You can *call* him in, or he'll come running under his own steam – once I've blown your brains out.'

Their eyes met again. Sweat pebbled the faces of both men. Finally Iniestra cleared his throat and nodded. 'All … all right,' he husked.

Roughly, so the Mexican would know he meant business, O'Brien pulled him away from the chest of drawers, spun him around and jabbed the muzzle of the pistol hard against his spine. 'No tricks, major,' he said, switching to Spanish. 'Just tell him to get in here. I'll handle the rest. Got it?'

'*Si.*'

O'Brien pushed him over to the door, reached around him, opened it and prodded him forward.

With his own gun stabbing him in the

kidneys, Iniestra said, 'Private Agustin! In here, quickly!'

O'Brien pulled the major back out of the doorway before the guard could get a closer look at him, then forced him to stand to one side. The guard, Agustin, hurried along the passage and into the room, his acne-scarred face expectant.

'*Si, jefe?*'

O'Brien didn't give him a chance to defend himself. Pouncing forward, he grabbed hold of the Marlin rifle, shoved it aside and lashed out with the handgun, pistol-whipping him with deadly efficiency.

Agustin's yelp died in his throat. His eyes rolled up in his head and he collapsed in a heap. Two bumps the side of large eggs strained to break through the skin covering his forehead.

'Why, you–'

O'Brien turned just as Iniestra lunged at him, batted his flailing arms aside and pistol-whipped him, too. Within moments the major had joined his subordinate on the floor.

Sticking the Lefauchex into his waistband, the blue-eyed soldier of fortune bent to check on the *rurales*. Their pulses were slow, their breathing deep. Unconscious, but otherwise unhurt. Good.

'*Madre de–!*'

O'Brien spun, the revolver back in his hand. Ramirez stood in the doorway, staring down the gun-barrel with eyes like saucers. 'No … no…'

O'Brien aimed the gun away from him and relaxed a shade. 'It's all right,' he said, sticking with Spanish. 'I don't kill men without reason. These two're unconscious, that's all.'

'*Si* … if … if you say so.'

'I say so.' O'Brien straightened to his full height and moved closer to the doctor. 'My wallet and handgun,' he said. 'Where are they?'

'The parlour,' Ramirez replied. 'The major … he … he told me to keep them there.'

O'Brien nodded. 'Let's go get 'em, then.'

'*Si* … *si*…'

Ramirez led him out of the bedroom, turned right and hurried around a corner. The parlour turned out to be a mean little room with two chairs, a table, a bookshelf (full, this time) and a portrait of President Gonzalez over the fireplace. The little medico rummaged in a drawer beneath the table and brought out the bill-fold. O'Brien's .38 Colt came next, wrapped inside his coiled gunbelt. Quickly he checked its load before buckling it on.

Ramirez watched him cross the room and lift his hat from a peg in the wall. When O'Brien came back to tower over him, he looked fit to faint.

'I'm leaving now,' O'Brien told him softly. 'Can I trust you not to raise the alarm?'

The medico nodded quickly. 'But … but of course.'

'I hope so,' O'Brien said in a flat voice. 'You patched me up, Ramirez, and I'm beholden. But if you *do* raise the alarm, so help me I'll come back and kill you. *Comprende?*'

Ramirez was too petrified to reply – which was exactly what O'Brien wanted. The poor sonofabitch could only bob his head.

Brushing past him, the fighting-man retraced his steps along the passage and glanced briefly into the room which contained the two unconscious *rurales*. Then he rounded another corner and came to the front door.

Pausing a moment, he drew in a deep breath. He was sweating harder than he should be; due, no doubt, to the fact that he'd started running before he was properly fit to walk.

But there was no time now for the luxury

of waiting until the queasy sensation rolling in his guts died down. There was no time for *anything* now except escape.

Reaching out, he opened the front door.

The plaza stretched ahead of him, shimmering in the sunlight. Heat bounced up off the ground to smack him in the face. Slowly, he panned his gaze from left to right. The only people he saw were civilians. Hearing a sound behind him, he turned.

Dr Ramirez looked up at him. 'Go, quickly,' the older man whispered urgently. 'The major ... he will not remain senseless forever.'

O'Brien nodded, still uncertain exactly where the doctor's sympathies really lay. Whether he was for or against Iniestra, though, he was right in what he'd said; if O'Brien was going to get out of Piedras Negras quietly, he was going to have to get out *quickly*.

'*Adios*,' he said, forcing his legs to carry him away from the doctor's home.

He crossed the plaza with his guts squeezed tight, fighting the urge to keep looking back over his shoulder. His first stop was the stable, where he settled his bill and had the gap-toothed ten-year-old saddle his quarterhorse. Leading the mount outside several minutes later, he mounted up and kicked the animal into a canter, reining in only when he reached the Hotel Isabel.

He'd paid a week in advance for the room, so they hadn't let it out to anyone else. As fast as he could without drawing undue attention, he claimed his key, climbed the stairs and let himself in, heaving a sigh of relief when he found his saddlebags, warbag and limited edition Winchester exactly where he'd left them a lifetime earlier.

Grabbing his gear, he hustled back downstairs and out through the reception. If he was lucky, he'd be back across the border in a short while, and his trouble here would be little more than–

'O'Brien!'

Somehow he fought against hauling iron as he spun around, for the street was moderately busy and he had no wish to start a shooting-match in which innocent by-standers might get hurt. It was just as well, too, because coming along the boardwalk towards him was the man who'd saved his life, Shep Morgan.

'Well if this don't beat all!' the big, homely-faced cowboy muttered, coming to a halt before him. 'Up an' about already, are you?' His squinting eyes travelled across

O'Brien's gear and a look of puzzlement replaced the smile on his long, dependable face. 'Lightin' out?' he asked quietly.

'Uh-huh.' O'Brien carried his gear along to the hitchrack at which he'd tethered his horse, and slipped the long gun into its sheath. Morgan followed him over.

'You know, I was figurin' to step on over to that doctor's place later an' see how you was doin',' he said in his slow Texan drawl. 'Care to share a little medicinal with me over to yonder *pulqueria* before you go?'

O'Brien turned to face him. 'Listen, Shep,' he said. 'I'm obliged to you for buying into that little fracas I had the other night. Figure that makes it *two* drinks I owe you. But I've really got to move. Some other time, maybe?'

'Sure,' Morgan replied easily. Seeing that O'Brien still looked a little rough, the big cowboy took his saddlebags from him and went over to buckle them behind the double-rig's cantle. 'You look awful beat to be movin', though,' he remarked.

O'Brien smiled mirthlessly. 'I'll look a damn-sight more beat if I stick around here.'

Morgan frowned beneath the shade thrown by his grey hat-brim. 'Like that, is it?'

O'Brien caught the disapproval in the

other man's voice as he looped the tie-string on his warbag over his saddlehorn, and suddenly felt compelled to set the record straight. After all, Morgan had saved his life. O'Brien didn't want him to think it hadn't been worth the effort. 'It's not like *anything*,' he said. ''Fact I'm on the same side as the folks who want to cause me grief, not that they'd believe it.'

'You'd better get goin' then, I guess,' the cowboy said distantly.

'I will,' said O'Brien. 'Now get on away from me before someone sees us together and figures we're in cahoots.'

Morgan moved ponderously back onto the boardwalk, where he took off his hat and scratched idly at his stubble-shaded head.

O'Brien untied his reins and pulled himself up into the saddle. Looking down at the other man and feeling guilty that he hadn't been able to repay his kindness, he said, 'Next time I'm up around Crystal City–'

'*Alto!*'

O'Brien's head snapped around fast. Four men in *rurale* uniform had appeared at the end of the street, a lieutenant and three privates. Shadows covered their swarthy faces, but the junior officer's tone was easy enough to understand, as were the Marlin rifles he and his men were pointing O'Brien's way.

'*Scat!*' hissed Morgan.

Pulling hard on the reins, he spun the horse on a dime and sent it blurring up the street, away from the local *policia*, just as one of the privates, perhaps more eager than the rest, slapped his rifle to his shoulder and fired a hasty shot.

Immediately the whole street erupted into a cacophony of screams and yells as the townsfolk quickly ran for cover. Again O'Brien yanked on the reins, swerving the quarter-horse to avoid colliding with the scampering *peones*.

Another shot blasted through the muggy four o'clock air, causing more sounds of distress. The lieutenant yelled at his men to cease fire, then called out for horses.

'*Cogelo – rapidamente!*'

O'Brien's horse thundered madly around the first corner it came to, and he did nothing to stop it. He had to put distance between himself and the *rurales* fast. But even as he got his first look at this new thoroughfare a curse fell from his lips.

The winding side-street hadn't been all that wide to begin with; on a market day, with stalls lining both pencil-thin sidewalks, it was more confining still.

The sound of the horse's clattering hooves bounced off the adobe walls rising to either side and carried out ahead, warning the shoppers to get out of the way. In an instant the occupants of this street, too, were transformed into a milling herd, panicked and panicking in their haste to get out of the crazy *gringo's* path.

About thirty yards ahead, three fat women squeezing through a gap between stalls accidentally toppled a stack of empty wicker baskets across the street. O'Brien drew back on the reins and the quarter-horse leapt the obstacle and continued running with hardly a break in stride.

An off-duty *rurale* who had been buying some food from a vendor at the corner of the street suddenly appeared in his path, handgun out and blasting.

'Halt, *hombre!*' he cried. '*Halt!*'

'The hell you say!' O'Brien yelled back.

The horse hit the *rurale* in the right shoulder and tossed him into the vendor's portable oven, spilling both onto their sides. Suddenly red-hot *tamales* were rolling all across the dusty sidewalk, and capering street urchins were appearing from out of nowhere to snatch them up.

O'Brien burst out of the side-street and cursed again when he realized that somehow, he'd come back into the plaza, and was heading smack-dab into another group of *rurales,* all of whom immediately began to point his way.

'*Ahi esta, teniente!* There he is!'

O'Brien yelled '*Whoa!*' and wrenched on the horse's reins. Snorting, the animal reared up onto its hind legs and twisted around. O'Brien's view of the faces in the crowd was suddenly replaced by the sky. Then the horse came back down onto all fours, shaking him up something torturous; a new set of curious and frightened faces replaced those of the *rurales;* and the horse was off again, tearing past the ornate well with the lieutenant and his detachment, now mounted, in hot pursuit.

Above the sound of the wind whipping past his ears O'Brien heard more gunfire, and bent lower over his horse's flying mane. By now the whole town had become alerted to the drama unfolding on its streets and most of the *peones* had retired to the boardwalks to watch the action in relative safety.

The high crack of handgun-fire shattered the late-afternoon tranquility, mingling with the cries of the pursuing *rurales,* who were

70

urging their horses to ever-greater speed.

They couldn't hope to outrun the quarter-horse, though – O'Brien hoped. The nameless animal had been built for speed. It chewed up the hard-packed dirt and left a billowing cloud of dust in its wake.

But still the *policia* stayed on his tail. And worse – they were finally starting to find their range.

Jamming his heels into the horse's belly to get more speed from the animal, O'Brien shot past the side-street to which he'd already brought chaos and continued on, on, along the tapering, twisted streets. He was beginning to feel nauseous again, but fought the urge to puke. Time enough for that later – always assuming there'd *be* a later, of course.

Then the cantinas, gambling-rooms and brothels on the fringes of the commercial district were behind him, and he was thundering between low, sand-coloured *jacales* again, no more than a hundred yards from the bridge back to Eagle Pass.

Gunfire crackled behind him. Bullets zipped past his head. Bouncing around in the saddle, he chanced a look over one shoulder. The lieutenant and his men were falling back a little, but showed no signs of

71

giving up the chase *just* yet.

He faced front again.

'Aw ... *shoot!*'

An old man in a sombrero and serape had led a *burro* and cart out of a side-alley some sixty feet ahead. The fellow had obviously been in a world of his own until the pounding of O'Brien's horse's hooves had made him look up. Now his eyes grew wide. His mouth opened. He muttered something soundless and fell to his knees.

'Get that thing out of the way!' O'Brien roared.

But the old man was transfixed by the rider bearing down on him, too terrified to move.

O'Brien's next curse was a sight more colourful.

The quarter-horse raced straight toward the cart on a course that could only end in collision. But at the last possible moment the animal leapt skyward, powered by rock-hard haunch muscles, and began to clear the cart by perhaps an inch, certainly no more.

For a moment O'Brien left the saddle, then came back into it with ball-mashing force. As he groaned and fought madly to keep from being thrown again, the horse caught one of its back legs on the way down, but only grazed it. It staggered, stumbled, righted itself and tore on, out of the town and across the rock-fringed trail back to the bridge.

Behind him, O'Brien heard the lieutenant yelling at the old man to shift his cart. He doubted that the *rurales* would be foolish enough to attempt to jump it, and he was right. That should buy him *some* time, at least.

Finally, rounding a bend in the trail, he came in sight of the bridge. Unable to control his elation, he let out a tired but triumphant whoop.

But then he saw the two *rurale* troopers blocking the Mexican side of the span and realized that he'd forgotten about the guards the authorities always stationed there.

'*Dammit!*'

Alerted by the gunfire, the troopers already had their rifles raised. One of them, a corporal, bellowed something to O'Brien about stopping.

But O'Brien had no intention of stopping. The lieutenant would be after him again in a while, so there could be no going back – only *forward*.

FOUR

O'Brien had a jarred view of the bridge speeding closer.

His ears filled with the cries of the men ahead, the drumming of the horse's hooves beneath him, the crash and babble of fast-flowing water sluicing under the wooden bridge.

'*Alto! Alto!*'

Reaching down, he pulled his Colt from leather.

As soon as the *rurales* saw him bringing the gun up, they quit chattering and tried to draw a bead on him. Before they could shoot, however, O'Brien squeezed the handgun's trigger.

The corporal screamed and dropped his rifle to the thick boards at his feet. Staggering, he clutched the bloody stain at his left shoulder as though to protect it from further harm.

Momentarily stunned, the trooper beside him wheeled around to gape as his superior sank, sobbing, to his knees.

Then the spell was broken and he snapped his attention back to the oncoming *gringo*.

By that time however, O'Brien was almost upon him; and deciding he was already too close to allow easy use of a long gun, the trooper up-ended the weapon, intending to use it as a club instead.

O'Brien saw him switch the Marlin around. He was loath to risk another shot in case he killed instead of wounded. He had no particular desire to cause any more suffering. The *policia* were only doing their duty, after all. But the trooper racing towards him now, with his face a map of rage and his makeshift club raised high, was still a threat, duty or not.

When no more than six feet separated them, O'Brien jerked on the reins and the horse slurred to a halt, momentum twisting its back-end a little to the right.

O'Brien had timed the move just right. The horse's hindquarters slammed the approaching trooper right in the chest and hurled him back where he came from. He fairly flew backwards, grunting once; then he hit the east-side guard-rail with the small of his back and somersaulted over the side.

O'Brien heard him scream; heard the splash he made striking the water; heard the subsequent sounds he made paddling awkwardly back to shore.

Then he set the horse into motion again and hastened across the bridge, back onto American soil.

Before the law in Eagle Pass could turn up at the bridge to see what all the fuss was about, O'Brien swung his horse away from the town, intending to lose himself for a while in the heavily-wooded hills to the east.

By the time early evening was streaking the cloudy sky he'd found a reasonable campsite close to a stream and off-saddled and picketed his horse close to some juicy bunch-grass.

He made a small fire, went through his possibles, fixed up some coffee and set a can of beans to cook through. Then he settled down with his saddle as a back-rest and allowed the last of the tension to slowly ease out of him.

For a moment back there, during his final climb into the hills, he'd half-expected to pass out. Every bone and muscle had seemed to start aching at once. But he'd lasted the journey out, and felt some better after stripping down and bathing in the cool, clear water of the stream.

He figured to improve still more once he got some good hot coffee and chow inside him, too. Reaching forward, he checked the progress of the meal. Already the beans had started to shift and bubble. The coffee was nearly done, too.

When at last he began to fork up the beans, his head had cleared sufficiently for him to review his position.

On the surface, of course, it seemed that he was no nearer to locating his target. But maybe Piedras Negras had proved to be a useful starting-point after all. Certainly, he'd stirred up a hornet's nest by asking around after the bandit, and he wasn't just thinking about Major Iniestra, either. His attackers, Baldy, Lard-Belly and the kid, were obviously in league with Angel. Why else would they have attempted to kill him otherwise?

It was possible, then, that *they* were the lead he was after.

But before he could question them further, he would have to go back into Piedras Negras and find them; and that could very well prove to be fatal.

He chewed the beans, swallowed, scooped up some more and thought about going back into Piedras Negras.

It would be tricky, all right.

But what the hell?

He didn't really have much of a choice.

He stayed put for the next couple of days, living off the land and what little supplies he had in his saddlebags. Slowly his bruises began to fade, his cuts and grazes to heal.

By the time he was ready to move out again, he felt just about as fit as he was likely to get. Saddling up, he checked his weapons, then pointed the quarter-horse southeast.

He followed the Rio Grande for about thirty miles, keeping his pace steady. By the time he reached the border town of Little Mesa, his beard, which had been growing untended ever since the *rurales* had hauled him into Ramirez' surgery, was thick enough to cover his square jaw and give him a vaguely different facial appearance. To further disguise himself, he bought a poncho, which would alter his body-shape.

After that, he was ready to cross back into Mexico, ride twenty miles to the south and west, then swing back northeast and approach Piedras Negras from behind.

At three o'clock that same afternoon, Sergeant Mata rapped smartly on the door marked with Major Iniestra's name. A moment later the major's voice said, 'Come in.'

Mata opened the door and took a pace into the room. He was a large man with a big stomach. Seeing Iniestra sitting at his desk, wading slowly through a sea of paperwork, he snapped a sharp salute and apologized for the intrusion.

The office was about fifteen feet square. Iniestra's desk, two chairs and a wooden file cabinet were the only items of furniture. A map of the country between Ciudad Acuna and Boquillas to Lampazos and Nuevo Laredo had been tacked up on the wall to the major's right. To his left, the Mexican flag had been draped across half a dozen nails in the wall. Behind him, sunlight streamed in through a large casement window.

'What is it, Mata?' Iniestra asked gruffly. He was still feeling sore from the pistol-whipping he'd received a few days earlier; his bumps and bruises were still pronounced.

'*Perdon, jefe,* but–'

Before the NCO could say anything more, two tall men in the pale grey-green uniform of the *federales* pushed past him and entered the room, their boots clattering loud on the bare floorboards. The eldest was perhaps fifty. He had a long, hollow face with a dusky complexion and, curious for a Mexican, dark-blue eyes beneath thick, snowy brows. His uniform bore the marks of travel; as he threw a glance at the sergeant, he slapped dust from his sleeve using the hand that wasn't holding his riding-crop.

The red band around the peaked caps of both men marked them as *colorados* – members of the elite and much-feared band of soldiers who operated within the ranks of the *federales*.

'That will be all, sergeant,' Iniestra said quietly.

Mata gulped and said, *'Si, jefe.'*

He beat a hasty retreat from the room.

Iniestra was not surprised to see the newcomers. He'd been expecting a visit from them ever since he'd dispatched his report on O'Brien's escape to Mexico City. Slowly he rose to his feet. 'Colonel Redarte,' he said, saluting.

The older man, Redarte, returned the acknowledgement carelessly, as if he had little time for military protocol. Then he gestured to his companion. 'This is my assistant, Captain Gerardo,' he said.

'Pleased to meet you, captain,' Iniestra said formally, hating himself for showing such deference to a junior officer.

Gerardo was a tall, thickset man in his late twenties or early thirties. He had a round, cheerless face and thinning black hair, heavy-lidded hazel eyes and fleshy lips turned down at the corners. He made no reply, save to take off his cap. He reminded Iniestra of the undertaker back home in Concepçion del Oro, where he had lived until joining the *rurales* in '61.

'Please ... take a seat, colonel.' Iniestra glanced around the room, perhaps hoping to find a third chair he had hitherto over-looked. 'Captain ... excuse me while I–'

'I'll stand,' said Gerardo.

'As ... as you will.'

Iniestra waited until Colonel Redarte had seated himself before doing likewise. Redarte took off his cap to reveal a thick mane of hair as grey as steel, swept back from a high, much-lined forehead.

'We came as soon as we received your report,' the colonel said slowly, while Gerardo sauntered around the desk to peer out the widow. 'It is, after all, a very serious matter.'

Iniestra nodded, growing uncomfortably aware of the captain hovering behind him. Gerardo's shadow spilled across the paperwork in front of him, blotting out the warmth of the sun on his back.

'It is regrettable that you did not appreciate exactly who this man O'Brien was,' Redarte went on, taking a slim silver case from his right breast pocket and helping himself to a dark-papered cigarette. 'Why, the *gringo* caused so much trouble the last time he was in Mexico that I thought he would be virtually impossible to forget.'

Iniestra licked his lips. 'His name seemed familiar...' he mumbled uncertainly.

'He is a freelance adventurer,' Gerardo supplied, hurrying back around the desk to scratch a match and hold it to Redarte's cigarette. 'You may remember that business down in Espina three years ago. An American politician was being held in prison on suspicion of murder.'

'Of course!' Iniestra cried, snapping his fingers. '*Now* I have it! This O'Brien – he came to help the *politico* escape, and killed a number of men from the border militia while he was at it.'

'One of your own fellow-officers, too,' Redarte said, exhaling a cloud of smoke into the air. 'Captain Hector Vadala.'

Iniestra felt his cheeks burning. To think that *he* had held the very man responsible in his grasp – and let him escape! He should have doubled the guard, taken O'Brien into custody as soon as–

But how was he to know? Espina was more than a hundred miles away, and three years was a long time. Besides, one *gringo* looked much the same as another to Iniestra.

Still, the *colorados* had remembered.

The *colorados* never forgot anything.

They wouldn't forget *this*.

'I have to be honest with you, major,' Redarte said, running his dark-blue eyes over the desk, searching in vain for an ashtray. 'We have long been hoping that this man would come south again, so that we might arrest him. Your inability to recognize him, however, further compounded by your inability to *hold* him, has called your competence into serious doubt.'

'But–'

Redarte held up his riding-crop to indicate silence. As Iniestra reluctantly closed his mouth, Gerardo held out his cupped left hand. Without batting an eyelid, the colonel flicked ash into it. 'You say O'Brien came here looking for that insurrectionist dog Angel Salazar?'

'*Sí, coronel.*'

'He told you this?'

'Not exactly.' Quickly Iniestra explained

83

about the events which had led to the attack on O'Brien.

'We don't know *exactly* why he was searching for the Angel, then?'

'No, *jefe*. I assumed that O'Brien was looking to join forces with him. Either that, or conduct some sort of business with him.'

'O'Brien came here alone?'

'Yes, colonel.'

'You're certain?'

Iniestra paused. 'I … yes, sir.'

'Then why did you hesitate?' asked Gerardo.

'I was just thinking,' the major said. 'The man who found O'Brien just after he'd been beaten up … he too is an American. Some of the people we questioned later said they saw him and O'Brien conversing just before O'Brien left town.'

'Could they be connected in some way, do you think?'

'I doubt it. This other *gringo,* his name is Morgan. He came to town with four or five others, about four days ago. They are *vaqueros,*' he said. 'Cowboys.'

'*Are* they?' asked Redarte. 'This Morgan, he is still in town?'

'So far as I know.'

'Arrest him, then. I'll question him. I

84

doubt that O'Brien will come back to Piedras Negras, but if he *does* want to find Salazar for some reason, his friend might know where he intends to turn up next.'

Iniestra said, 'With respect, colonel, I think you'll be wasting your time with Morgan. The man is nothing to O'Brien, I'm sure. He–'

'Arrest him, major,' said Gerardo, with no consideration for rank. 'Straight away. The colonel will want him detained and ready for questioning by four o'clock, is that understood?'

Major Iniestra's dark-brown eyes focused on the desk-top and his voice lowered in volume. He, like any sensible man, knew better than to anger the *colorados*. The bastards! They intimidated everyone. 'I … I'll see to it myself,' he muttered, rising. 'At once.'

O'Brien encountered no-one as he angled his horse deeper into Mexico. Towns were few and far between, and the dry, yucca-patched flatlands did not encourage farmers or ranching.

But the isolation suited him fine as the miles unwound beneath him and slowly he began to turn his horse from southwest to west, to northwest and finally north.

It took him just under two days to reach Piedras Negras. When he did he reined in about half a mile outside the town limits and well back from any recognized trails leading in from the south. He unbit the quarter-horse and allowed it to graze, and opened a can of peaches for himself. Then, nestled in among a comfortable screen of paloverde trees and rocks, he sat waiting for nightfall.

The three men he was after had first sighted him at a cantina known as Pablo's. That was where he would search for them tonight. That they were local men he had no doubt. Oh, they were proficient-enough fighters, sure, but he had a feeling they were townsmen all the same; men who had to content themselves by merely *supporting* the bandit from afar. Gang-members would have most likely taken O'Brien straight to the Angel himself, and let *him* decide O'Brien's fate. Baldy and his comrades had taken matters into their own hands, which implied that while they might know how to contact the bandit, they had no easy access to him.

The blue-eyed soldier of fortune felt similarly confident about going back into the town. It was, after all, the last place anyone would expect to find him. His beard, plus the poncho, were extra insurance against being recognized.

Still, he'd remain wary, just in case. After all these years, caution was in his blood.

The blue sky slowly turned to grey. Salmon-coloured clouds streaked across the heavens. Full dark descended slowly, and Piedras Negras began to light up with a hundred or more lanterns. From this distance he made out little until a cloud shifted away from the moon. Then he saw the pale, clustered adobes, gradually rising in height as they crowded toward the centre of town.

Eight o'clock turned to nine, nine to ten, ten into ten-thirty.

O'Brien crushed out his fifth cigarette of the evening and mounted up.

He entered town sometime around a quarter to eleven. Most of the *jacales* were in darkness, their occupants asleep. The deeper he went into the centre of town, however, the more signs of life he saw.

Dropping his shoulders and slouching lower in the saddle, he kept his head down and his eyes restless. A few *peones* hurried down the street and past him. Here he spotted a *rurale* trooper on patrol, there a couple more, off-duty and obviously in high spirits.

Joining the light flow of *burro-* and wagon-traffic clattering across the moon-washed plaza, he noticed that lamps still burned within the *rurale* headquarters to his left. As bold as brass, he skirted the central fountain and rode right past the building, no more than thirty feet from it.

That was when the main door opened and two tall men in pale grey-green uniform stepped out into the night. He threw a seemingly casual glance their way. They were in conversation and paid him no mind. He saw the red bands on their caps, however, and realized that Iniestra was having to entertain two of *El Presidente's colorado* butchers.

Keeping his horse to a walk, he moved on, into the all-concealing shadows.

When at last he found himself alone in a side-street not far from Pablo's, he reined in and dismounted. Tying his horse to a hitch-rack in front of a closed-up butchery, he slipped his Winchester from leather and cradled it in his arms. The poncho covered the long gun admirably.

Developing a stoop and shuffle, O'Brien worked his way nearer the town's red-light district, listening not only to the sounds of pianos and guitars, of laughter, cat-calls and the clink of glass against glass, but also to the fainter night-noises beyond the general merriment; the sounds of cats prowling, dogs barking, a couple arguing, babies crying and *paisanos* rooting optimistically through other folks' garbage.

When Pablo's came into sight on the other side of the street, O'Brien pulled up and glanced both ways. The street was empty but for a dark-haired woman smoking a cigarette sixty yards away. He watched her for a moment, then returned his attention to the squat, solid bulk of the cantina opposite.

Butter-coloured light shone out through the windows to either side of the entrance. Narrowing his eyes, O'Brien made out figures milling around inside, and heard the buzz of chatter, the wild, uneven wail of a trumpet in the hands of one who obviously could not play it.

He crossed the street.

Standing to one side of the window just right of the closed cantina door, he peered inside. The glass was fly-blown and dusty, but clean enough to afford him a good field of vision. Smoke hung around the low ceiling, turning the lamplight hazy. Sweaty men and women showed an endless variety of teeth in loose, drunken grins. He scanned the occupants of the tables scattered around the place, those congregated around the sweet-smelling puddles on the bar.

He did not see the men he was after.

'*Hola, gringo.* You lookin' for comp'ny, *si?*'

O'Brien wheeled around and came face to face with the woman who moments before had been standing further along the street. Up close he put her age at thirty or so. She was tall and thin, with high cheekbones and a wide mouth. Her eyes were dark and alluring, her hair long, black and centre-parted. She wore a dress of some deep red colour, low-cut to reveal the valley between her small breasts. Her shoulders were covered in a black shawl.

'No company,' he said softly. 'Thanks all the same.'

She finished her cigarette, dropped the glowing amber end earthward and crushed it out with the sole of one cheap sandal. 'I can be *good* comp'ny,' she insisted.

'I believe it. But not right now, okay?'

She shrugged, turned, began to amble slowly back up the street towards her crib.

O'Brien spent a moment watching her go, then turned back to the cantina window. A sea of swarthy faces met his searching gaze, but all of them were the faces of strangers.

On impulse he turned back to the re-treating whore. 'Hey, *querida. Uno momento!*'

She was thirty feet away. Quickly he caught up to her. A knowing smile played across her thin face. Such a power it was she had over the opposite sex! But O'Brien hadn't succumbed to her dubious charms, as she soon found out.

'*Querida,*' he said. 'I'm trying to find three men.'

She looked disappointed. 'I know *mucho* men.'

'That's what I'm counting on.' Edging her towards the shadows, he started to describe the trio he was after in a series of sharp whispers. 'The first is tall, around forty, completely bald but for a thick black beard. The second–'

'You talk of Alfonso Sanchez,' she cut in quietly.

'You know him?'

Mischief played in her dark eyes. '*Well.*'

'What about his friends? A shorter, heavier man with a round face and a hooked nose, and a kid, good-looking, favours black duds?'

'That would be Emilio and Fortino.'

'Where can I find them?'

'How much is it worth?'

There was no time to haggle. He released his right-handed grip on the Winchester under the poncho and pulled a double eagle from his pants-pocket. 'This much,' he said.

The coin seemed to hold her transfixed. In an instant she had reached up to take it. 'Come,' she said. 'I will take you to them.'

'No tricks,' he warned. 'And no noise. These men, if they see me before I see them, they'll try to kill me. So tread carefully. One false move and you'll be the first to die.'

She took the threat without flinching. 'I understand.'

'You have a name?' he asked.

'Elvira.'

'All right, Elvira; lead on.'

She did; away from Pablo's, across the virtually-deserted street and down a long, twisting alleyway redolent with the smells of urine and rat-crap.

'Just where are we going?' he asked after a while.

'To find the men you are seeking.'

'I know that. What I mean is, where exactly are we *headed?*'

'A gambling-den,' she said without looking at him. 'Alfonso and his cronies can always be found there.' A new thought suddenly occurred to her, and she turned her head to study him briefly. 'Alfonso is a bad man to tangle with, *gringo*. He has powerful friends. Cross him, and you dig your own grave.'

Suddenly she slowed down and came to a halt at the mouth of the alley. 'We are here,' she whispered.

The alley opened out into another narrow thoroughfare. *Jacales* shelved away to both sides of the rutted dirt road. All but one was in darkness. That was the one Elvira pointed out.

'*Ahi*,' she hissed. 'There.'

O'Brien studied the place thoughtfully. It was drab and single-storeyed. A babble of conversation issued from one open window, the topic cards, women and the price of corn. 'You're sure I'll find them in there?' he asked. 'If you're lying–'

'You'll find them,' she predicted. 'Fortino's uncle owns the place. They frequent it because their drinks are always on the house.'

O'Brien glanced at the whore, wondering how far he could trust her. 'All right,' he said at last, digging out another coin. 'Not a word to anyone about this, all right?'

'*Si.*'

'*Gracias, querida.* You'd better get out of here now.'

She didn't need telling twice. '*Que tengas*

93

suerte, gringo,' she said with a wink. 'Good luck.'

Then she drifted quietly back the way she had come.

O'Brien stayed where he was, considering his next move. He had no wish to cause a fuss. He wanted to get as much information from his three targets as quickly and as quietly as possible, then get out of town before there was any more trouble with the *rurales*.

Going into the gambling-den was out of the question, then. He would have to wait for Baldy – Alfonso – and his friends to come out.

With the shadows cloaking him, he stood just back from the alley-mouth, watching the gambling-den.

The minutes ticked by. It must be half-past eleven now. He wondered if he'd been wrong to put his trust in the whore. Then the door to the gambling-den swung open and three men spilled out onto the street. O'Brien stiffened, then relaxed when he realized they weren't the men he was after.

The gamblers said their goodnights, oblivious to his presence so near. Two of them headed west, the other east.

O'Brien's sigh was soft but expressive.

He took his left hand away from the Winchester barrel and wiped his palm on his pants. He was just about to do the same with his right when he heard a faint sound coming from somewhere far behind him.

'*Shhh!*'

He turned, trying in vain to pierce the shadows. Apart from some dark bulks which he'd seen on the way here and indentified as stacks of uncollected garbage, he saw nothing. After that warning shush, he *heard* nothing either.

But he didn't need to. That one and only sound had been enough.

Someone was coming down the alleyway, desperately trying to keep quiet in the hopes of taking him by surprise.

O'Brien brought his long gun out from beneath the poncho and prepared to meet whoever it was head-on.

It looked like it was going to be a night for surprises.

FIVE

It took them six minutes to get within twelve feet of the alleymouth. Then one of them made a sound of surprise, and another said, 'There's nobody here!'

The third man, Alfonso Sanchez, said, 'You're sure this is where you left him, Elvira?'

'Of course!'

'Then where is he now?'

The second figure shifted in the darkness. He looked paunchy, round-faced, hook-nosed, and he wore a wide-brimmed sombrero. That was Emilio, then; otherwise known as Lard-Belly. His right arm, the one O'Brien had broken during their first encounter, was cradled in a sling.

'Is this some kind of trick, *puta?*' he demanded. 'Did the *gringo* put you up to this?'

Elvira registered surprise. 'No trick! I–'

He lashed out with a slap that echoed in the confines of the alley. 'If you're lying to us–'

'I'm not!' she cried hotly. 'Perhaps he went

96

into Duarte's place to try and find you!'

The first of the male figures moved into a stray shaft of moonlight. For just a moment his smooth, handsome face was revealed clearly. 'Perhaps he did,' the kid allowed, addressing Alfonso in the manner of a trusted adviser.

'But then again,' said O'Brien, choosing that exact moment to step out from behind one of the litter-strewn alley's many tall mountains of refuse, 'maybe I didn't.'

All four silhouettes spun around at the soft sound of his voice, then came up sharp when they saw him standing no more than ten feet away from them, his Winchester held at hip-height and pointed their way.

'Well, well, well,' O'Brien said into the silence.

Elvira swallowed a nervous sob and Alfonso, recovering first, tried a bluff by asking him who he was and what he wanted.

'I think you already know the answers to both those questions, *cabron*,' O'Brien replied, his voice suddenly hardening. 'Now, all of you, turn around and put your hands up against the wall.'

The kid chanced a step forward, black eyes furious. 'The hell you say!'

O'Brien moved in fast, a fleeting shadow

in the gloom, and let the kid have the Winchester stock right alongside the face. Elvira called his name, Fortino, but Fortino didn't hear it. With a grunt, his eyes rolled up into his head and he tumbled backwards into the dirt.

'*Bastardo!*' spat Alfonso, moonlight shining on his bald dome.

Spinning, O'Brien jammed the barrel of the rifle into his belly. 'Turn around!' he repeated. 'All of you! Hands up high, flat to the wall!'

While they did as he'd told them, muttering darkly, O'Brien glanced both ways along the alley. The gambling-den's meagre light didn't penetrate this far, so they were hidden from view. But he didn't want to push his luck; just get some answers and then get out of there.

When Alfonso, Emilio and Elvira were facing the wall, O'Brien stared at each back in turn. Only the whispery sounds of their breathing filled the shadow-thick thoroughfare, that and the occasional patter-patter of a rat scurrying back and forth in the darkness.

'I want the Angel,' O'Brien said at last. 'And you're going to tell me where I can find him.'

Alfonso chanced a look over his right shoulder. 'You're *loco!*' he said, his thick black beard wagging in time to the words. 'I don' even know what you're–'

O'Brien slammed the Winchester stock into the small of his back, tearing a groan from him. 'I don't have the time to play games with you,' he said. 'And considering how close you fellers came to killing me the other night, I don't need any encouragement to play rough. Now – where do I find the Angel?'

'He doesn't know!' hissed Elvira.

'No? What about *you,* Emilio? What do *you* know?'

'*Nothing!*' the sombrero-wearing hardcase spat harshly.

'Too bad,' said O'Brien. Lifting the Winchester again, he brought the stock down against the nape of the other man's neck with enough force to pole-axe him. Emilio gasped, clawed at the wall with his one good hand, then slid down into a puddle of something foul.

O'Brien returned his attention to Alfonso and the whore. Alfonso might be a hard man, but even he was shocked by O'Brien's savagery and apparent lack of mercy.

'Feeling talkative yet, Alfonso?' O'Brien

asked pleasantly.

'Go to hell, *hijo de puta!*'

O'Brien stepped back from the taller man, transferred his rifle from his right hand to his left, then crouched over Emilio's sprawled form and pulled the man's machete from the sheath hanging on his weapons-belt.

Alfonso's eyes bulged as O'Brien straightened back up. They moved from his face to the blade, then back to his face. O'Brien smiled without humour as he slowly raised the machete high above his head.

'Ever wondered what life could be like for a man with no hands, *cabron?*' he asked.

Alfonso squinted at him, trying to decide whether or not he was bluffing.

'Let's see, shall we?' O'Brien suggested. 'We'll start with the fingers of your right hand, then work our way down to the wrist.'

Elvira started trembling. 'Tell him, Alfonso! For the love of God–'

'*Callarte!* Shut up!'

'But he *means* it, Alfonso...'

O'Brien tensed his right arm in preparation for the first blow, secretly hoping that the big bald man wouldn't call his bluff. 'Well?' he demanded tightly.

Sweat stood out on Alfonso's forehead. His dark eyes looked haunted. 'He'll kill me if I tell you,' he muttered.

'*I'll* kill you if you don't,' O'Brien reminded him.

'It's Maria you want!' Both men discarded their eyeball-match to look at Elvira, who had twisted away from the wall, desperate to tell everything so long as Alfonso didn't lose his hands. 'Maria Oropeza!'

'Who's she?'

'She's the Angel's girl.'

'She lives here?'

'*Si*. Maybe three blocks to the south.'

'Shut up, *puta!*' snarled Alfonso.

O'Brien's eyes flicked back to the bald man. '*You* shut up,' he said.

And brought the machete down.

The woman screamed, but there was no need. O'Brien cracked Alfonso on the skull with the handle of the long knife, not the blade. The bald man cursed, sank to his knees, fought to rise again. Hating himself for it, O'Brien hit him once more, and this time Alfonso plunged into unconsciousness.

'All right,' he said, tossing the machete aside with a cold, metallic clang. 'Take me to this girl, Elvira. But so help me, try to play me false again and I'll skin you alive!'

This time the whore *did* react to his verbal threat. Already trembling, she bobbed her

101

head, eager to convince him of her sincerity. 'No tricks,' she sobbed. 'No tricks.'

'Let's move, then.'

Grabbing his right hand, she led him back along the alley, past shapeless hulks of moon-silvered trash and puddles of urine, out onto the main street, left, across the thoroughfare and down another alley. Dogs barked. Cats cried like babies. A few *peones* strolled on the pencil-thin sidewalks, but O'Brien and the whore managed to avoid them.

'Tell me about this Maria Oropeza,' O'Brien said as they hurried on through the midnight blackness.

'What is there to tell?' Elvira asked with a shrug in her voice. 'She was a sporting girl, like so many of us, until the Angel came into her life. Then she gave it up, and went to work in her aunt's bakery.'

The envy in her tone was unmistakable.

'The Angel comes to visit her?' O'Brien prodded. That would certainly agree with Captain Taylor's guess.

The girl confirmed it with a nod. 'Whenever he can. But don't expect Maria to betray her man without a fight, *gringo*. You'll have to beat her before she'll tell you where to find him.'

'It won't come to that,' O'Brien said absently, already settling on his next course of action.

'No?' Elvira asked in spite of herself. 'How so?'

'Because as soon as the Angel hears that I've taken his girl hostage,' he replied calmly, 'I figure he'll come and find *me*.'

'You're crazy!' the whore spat in disbelief.

And maybe he was. But assuming everything she'd told him about Maria and the Angel was true, it was his best bet for luring the bandit into his sights – providing he could pull it off, that was.

Elvira fell silent now that she knew his intention. He glanced down at her grim profile. She was probably wondering what kind of a sumbitch he was to pistol-whip three men, threaten to cut the hands off one and then snatch a defenceless woman from her own home just to use as bait to kill her lover. And putting it that way, O'Brien began to feel even lousier about himself than he already did.

Without warning, his thoughts turned to Shep Morgan. Lord alone knew what the big, neighbourly cowboy must've thought of him, lighting out with the *rurales* on his tail.

Suddenly Elvira came to a halt, bringing

him back to full awareness. 'We're there,' she said.

The *jacal* some twenty feet ahead of them looked ghostly in the moonlight. Shadowy pits marked the positions of its windows and door, and some little distance beyond the place he discerned the poles of a small corral. Glancing up and down the street, he saw a number of commercial enterprises, now locked-up for the night.

'Maria lives in there alone?' he asked.

Without meeting his gaze, doubtless shamed by her betrayal, Elvira only nodded.

'All right,' he said, turning to face her. 'Now listen to me. I don't care how you do it, but get word to the Angel fast. Tell him I've got his girl, and if he wants her back, he'll come alone to *Picar Cumbre* at noon five days from now. *Comprende?*'

'*Picar Cumbre...*' Elvira repeated, fixing the name of Needle Peak, an easily-defensible rocky outcrop some forty miles to the south, in her memory. 'All ... all right. I will do ... what I can.'

'I know you will,' he said. She'd be too scared to do otherwise.

Now came the most difficult part for O'Brien. She'd already shown that she couldn't be trusted. If he let her go, she'd

104

head straight for friends of Alfonso and the others, and raise the alarm.

She, too, must be silenced for a while, then.

Careful not to telegraph his intention, he set his Winchester to one side; then, when she least expected it, he lashed out with confounding speed, clipping her on the jaw.

She gave a small sound of surprise, a kind of half-swallowed gulp, then began to fall.

O'Brien caught her before she hit the ground, and swept her up in his arms. He told himself that he'd had no choice but to strike her, but that didn't stop him from feeling any less of a bastard. Critically he studied her face in the soft, uncertain light. If you ignored the bruise smudging her jaw, she might just have been sleeping.

He set her down in the deepest shadows of the alley they'd just come from, and covered her with her black shawl. She should be safe enough there; if anyone spotted her before she woke up of her own accord, they'd likely dismiss her as nothing more than a drunk.

He still felt bad about hitting her, though.

Slipping the Winchester back under his poncho, he quickly retraced his steps across the dark, sleeping town, sweating hard now, and fearful that Alfonso and his cronies might begin to regain consciousness too soon, until he came to the side-street in which he'd tethered his horse.

Thrusting the long gun back into its sheath, he mounted up and kicked the animal into a trot, reining back only when he reached the spot at which he'd left the heavy-breathing Elvira.

Dismounting and ground-hitching the horse, O'Brien cast another anxious glance up and down the street. It was still quiet – and he still had misgivings about the plan he'd embarked upon. But there was no time for dallying now. He had to get on with it, and hope for the best.

Hurriedly he crossed the uneven trail and listened for a moment at the *jacal* door.

The hiss of silence met his ears.

Drawing in a deep breath, he rapped softly on the unplaned wood. Nothing. Again he knocked, waiting expectantly. No answer.

He was just about to knock a third time when a muffled voice on the other side of the portal asked who was there.

O'Brien froze for a moment. 'Maria?' he said in an urgent whisper, 'Maria Oropeza?'

'Who is it?' asked the girl on the other side of the door. She sounded tired, scratchy, curious and afraid.

'The Angel sent me,' he lied in Spanish. 'Open up now, quickly!'

For a second or two there was nothing, not even the heavy sound of her still-sleepy breathing, to be heard. O'Brien bit on his lower lip, wondering if she'd seen through his attempted ruse.

Then there came the sawing sound of a bolt being pulled back, and the door opened a crack. He saw one dark eye, a blemish-free cheek, one half of a pair of generous, sensual lips.

She looked very, very young.

'The Angel?' she echoed, studying his dark silhouette warily.

He nodded, seeing a look in her eye, a sense of anticipation she was unable to disguise. Elvira had been telling it straight, then. Maria *was* the Angel's girl. From the look of her, she fairly worshipped him.

'He sent me to fetch you,' O'Brien hissed.

'He's *here?*'

'Waiting just outside town.'

She thought about that for a moment, then said, 'He's all right? There's been no trouble?'

'No trouble,' he replied. 'He just wanted to see you.'

'You'd better come in then,' she said,

swinging the door wider, 'while I get dressed.'

'Hurry,' he said, stepping into a small, simply-furnished room that appeared stark black-and-white in the gloom.

She hustled across the room with her nightgown billowing around her. Her movements were so silent and graceful that she might have been a floating phantom. Just before she disappeared into the bedroom she said, 'You're new.'

'What?'

'I've never seen you before.'

'I've only been with the Angel for a month.'

He heard the sounds she made stepping out of the nightgown and pulling a dress over her head. 'You have a name?' she asked, her high voice muffled by cotton.

'Carter,' he said. It was no lie.

'The Angel must trust you,' she said. 'To have sent you to fetch me.' There was a pause. 'I'm glad. Some of his men ... it was a mistake to have ever taken them on.'

He glanced around the spartan room, taking no pleasure from his deception. 'Have you got a horse I could be saddling?' he asked.

'*Sí.* Out back. A colt.' She appeared in the bedroom doorway, hands fixing the buttons at the back of what looked like a fine blue dress. Through the darkness he saw the bright flash of her teeth. 'Angel gave him to me,' she explained proudly.

He forced himself to smile back. 'Nice,' he commented, moving across to the kitchen area. 'Does this door lead out back?'

'*Si*. All the saddle-gear is stacked just outside. I won't be long, Carter.'

He opened the back door, stepped out into the sharp, starry night and released a sigh. So far, so good, he thought. But there was still a long way to go. He spotted the colt standing on the other side of the corral, then glanced around until he found her saddle-gear.

Hefting it across to the horse, he began to ready the animal for travelling. She favoured the basic, small Eastern saddle most cowboys disparagingly called the pimple. It was designed for side-saddle riding, and didn't take long to cinch up. By the time the colt was ready to ride, so was Maria Oropeza.

Hearing her close the back door behind her, he turned and watched her hurry across to him. The sense of expectancy on her shadowy face was easy to read. It showed in the way she had chosen to wear her best dress, too. He caught the scent of lily of the

109

valley on her and stifled a vague sense of self-loathing.

Then she took the reins from him and he helped her up into the saddle. 'Where is *your* horse?' she whispered.

'Out front.'

He led her to the gate in the small corral's south-east wall, opened it and waited while she walked the colt out into the alley beside her *jacal*. Then he closed the gate and trotted back to where he'd left the quarter-horse. By the time he'd stepped up to leather, she was sitting her colt out front of her adobe hut.

'He is far?' she asked, referring to Angel.

'Not far,' O'Brien lied. 'A little to the south.' He nudged his horse into motion. 'Come on; I'll take you to him.'

She followed him without question, like a lamb to the slaughter, which meant that she was either incredibly naïve or so besotted with her lover that the thought of seeing him – even at one o'clock in the morning – had blinded her to all else.

'For an American,' she said, 'you have good Spanish.'

He shrugged. 'Thanks.'

'I mean it.'

Around them, the streets of Piedras Negras

were still and dozy. The only people they saw were drunks being tossed out of cantinas, and the odd, patrolling rural policeman, whose prime objective was to ensure that they caused no trouble.

When they reached the plaza, it was in darkness. The fountain at its centre seemed to spew liquid silver. Then black alleyways crowded them in again, until the low, sand-coloured *jacales* O'Brien had encountered on the way in told him that they'd reached the town's southern limits.

'Is it much further?' Maria asked impatiently.

He pitied her devotion to one so twisted. 'Not far.'

'*How* far?'

'Maybe half a mile.'

'You don't have much to say for yourself,' she remarked with a pout.

'That's because I haven't got much worth saying,' he replied, keeping his eyes peeled for trouble.

The town was behind them now, and flat, open prairie spread away to the east, south and west. Here a stand of Joshua trees clawed heavenward. There a mesa rose dark against the hazy purple horizon. O'Brien kept them headed south, his target the black,

111

undulating hills forty miles away.

'Are we there yet?' Maria asked, breaking in on his thoughts.

'Not yet.'

'That's what you said twenty minutes ago!'

He felt her eyes burning into his profile and knew that she was finally starting to realize that something was wrong.

'Where is the Angel?' she asked, her voice trembling with a mixture of fear and anger.

He didn't reply.

'You...' Her voice dried up and she had to start again. 'Angel didn't send you, did he?'

He reined in and she followed suit automatically. When he finally turned to face her, his .38 Colt was in his hand. 'No,' he said. 'Angel didn't send me.'

She stared into the gun-barrel with her mouth forming a tunnel of shock. Then her eyes moved back up to his face and he said, 'Now – shut up and do as I tell you, Maria ... or else.'

She was twenty-three years old and her heart-shaped face was framed by straight, shoulder-length, raven-black hair. She had narrow eyebrows above large, hazel eyes, the small, up-tilted nose of a child and the full, pouting lips of an experienced woman. Her blue dress was cut tight to her waist, and flared provocatively from her hips. She was maybe five feet seven, a hundred and ten pounds, slim, firm, desirable.

All this O'Brien finally got to see when the sun began to climb skyward four or five hours later. Then, with the sky gradually shifting from black to grey to white to blue, he glanced across at her and saw for the first time the woman he had kidnapped.

After he'd put his gun away, they'd ridden on in silence. Once he'd sensed a sudden electricity about her, as if she might be planning something reckless, and he'd said, 'Don't.'

She hadn't.

But that was the only conversation they'd had.

It had been a long night, and O'Brien was tired. But at least the hills to the south were twenty-five miles closer. If his calculations were right, they should reach *Picar Cumbre,* Needle Peak, around noon.

The deadening Mexican landscape stretched away to all sides of them now, barren and forbidding. Low white clouds hung like polka dots in the sky, looking down on shaggy beaked yucca plants, candelillas projecting stick-like from the cracked grey earth and strange, man-shaped cacti.

About an hour after sun-up they came to a shallow-running *riachuelo* bordered by dying clusters of sweet laurel and trinity plants, and O'Brien called a halt. He felt glassy-eyed and heavy-headed, and craved a cup of coffee to help chase away the last of the night's cold.

Dismounting, he told Maria to do likewise. At first she ignored him and stayed where she was. Then, because she too felt weary and saddle-sore, she decided to slide down beside him.

O'Brien took a small pot and a sack of beans from one of his saddlebags and held them out to the girl, saying, 'Gather some brush we can use for kindling while I take care of the horses.'

'Go to hell!' she spat.

But she took the pot and beans.

O'Brien led the animals to the stream, allowed them to water, then hobbled them on a yellow patch of needle-grass to graze. When he rejoined Maria, she had filled the pot with water, added beans and was waiting for him to start a fire.

Later, when the rich aroma of Arbuckle's lifted onto the gentle northerly breeze, they sat beside the narrow thread of chuckling water and blew on their steaming mugs. The sun was higher now, and stronger. Most of the clouds had been burned away.

'Who *are* you, Carter?' Maria asked in a cracked voice. 'What is it that you hope to gain by holding me against my will? Money? You think Angel will pay ransom for my return?'

He didn't look at her, but he guessed it was about time he came clean. Quietly he said, 'Oh he'll pay all right. But not with money, Maria. With *himself.*'

She digested that. 'You're a bounty-hunter,' she guessed.

He didn't reply.

'And you're going to use me to get him.'

'Something like that.'

She caught her breath suddenly, as something occurred to her. 'You are the man who caused so much trouble in the town a few days ago,' she said over the rim of her mug. 'The one the *rurales* chased. I heard about that. They say *he* was after my Angel, too.'

That she should be so fiercely protective of such a madman puzzled him, and he eyed her sidelong. 'What's the matter with you, Maria: Doesn't it bother you that Angel's a thief and a killer? That he and his men rob and rape and murder whenever the mood takes them?'

Her heart-shaped face registered indignation. She shook her head, sending a shiver through her glistening blue-black hair. 'It would if it were true,' she snapped, hoarse with rage. 'But it isn't. It's a lie,'

'It's the truth,' he stated in a flat voice. 'And you know it.'

She stared off across the stream, her eyes reflecting the sunlight sparkling on the water's surface. 'Oh, I know all about what you *say* are the Angel's crimes,' she muttered in a low voice. 'But would it do me any good to tell you that you're wrong? That my Angel is blameless? That he–' She broke off, and fixed him with a look of disgust so strong that he almost recoiled from it. 'But what is the use? You do not want to know the truth, *gringo*. You want only the blood money you'll collect on Angel's carcass!'

'It's not like–'

But before he could finish his denial, she leapt into action, suddenly hurling the steaming contents of her mug straight in his face, screaming when he fell back, and pushing herself up and away from him.

O'Brien couldn't stop the yelp of surprise that burst from his lips. She'd caught him completely unawares, and now he was paying for it. His hands came up to his scalded face, he muttered a few choice curses, he pawed the coffee out of his eyes and powered up onto his feet and after her.

She hadn't gone far. She'd made it to the horses and was struggling to remove the hobbles on the colt, but that was all. Then she heard the sounds he made blundering up the sloping stream-bank and through the swaying needle-grass, turned to stare into his blotchy, sore-looking face, cried out and forgot all about her horse, just started running, trying to outdistance him on foot.

He raced after her, trying to push the pain of his burned skin to the back of his mind. His eyes were misty; he squeezed them shut for a second, to clear them. Up ahead, no more than forty feet away, Maria tore across the grey desert floor as fast as her full, rustling dress would allow. O'Brien heard the small sobs she made breathing, heard his own breath rasping in his ears.

He yelled her name again, told her to stop. It came as no surprise when she completely ignored him. Then she stumbled a bit, and he got the impression that she'd accidentally stepped on the hem of her dress. He watched her tumble forward, heard her scream–

–and saw something cold and reptilian slither
through the short, tufty grass towards her.
He pulled up sharp, in shock.
'Maria – get up, quickly!'
But it was too late.
The snake was already upon her.

SIX

Her scream came shrill and terrified as the disturbed snake, an ugly-looking black-tailed rattler, wriggled towards her in a series of fluid, S-shaped movements.

She screamed again when the thing struck out, unnerved by the threshing of her arms and legs, and sank its fangs into her left hand.

Maria rolled over, panic making her movements jerky and desperate. The rattler went with her, loath to release its grip. As O'Brien surged across the ground towards her, she shook her arm, hoping to hurl the snake away, but still it clung to her, the black eyes beneath its fused eyelids curiously dead as it whipped this way and that.

O'Brien estimated the snake to be at least four feet long, with a thick, scaly body the colour of mud, marked with black diamond shapes and a distinctive black tail.

Reaching the struggling girl, he thrust his right hand down at the spot just behind the rattler's flat head, grabbed it, squeezed–

119

The snake's jaws opened at last.

Amidst all the chaos, O'Brien saw the thin holes just beneath the knuckles of Maria's left little finger. The blood welled up from them and the snake began coiling itself around his right arm like some sort of bizarre living bracelet.

He turned away from the girl, still gripping the snake by its neck. Its jaws snapped twice. He saw venom dripping freely from its gaping maw and quickly put his head back to avoid the slashing black rattle chattering past his right ear.

He crouched, somehow managed to get the snake's unblinking head flat to the ground, stamped his foot on it and tried to drag his arm out from between its throbbing curls.

But the rattler increased its grip still further, furious now. O'Brien felt the meat of its body plain through the sleeve of his shirt and fought down a shudder of revulsion.

With his left hand, he reached behind him and fumbled his jack-knife from one hip pocket. The snake wriggled like a mad thing as it tried to twist out from beneath his boot. He opened the knife, positioned it just behind the reptile's brain, held it there for a moment, then thrust down.

All at once the rattler's limbless body constricted. O'Brien winced at the sudden increase of pain in his arm. He slammed the knife deeper into the snake, until he felt the blade begin to slide into the dry, crumbly earth beneath it, groaning a little more as the reptile swelled still further.

An eternity later, the rattler's struggles began to lessen, the deafening clack-clack-clack of its tail to slow like a dying heartbeat.

A moment later the snake gave one final convulsion, then fell away from his arm.

O'Brien stumbled backwards, turned and loped across to Maria. The girl lay on her back. Her face was moist with tears and she was moaning something that sounded very much like a prayer.

She jumped when he touched her shoulder, came out of her stupor and stared at him with dull, sick-looking eyes. *'El serpiente–!'* she began.

'It's dead,' he said, easing her momentary panic with the news. 'Now lay still. The more you shift about, the further you'll pump the poison around your body.'

When that penetrated her agitation she froze, squinting up at the sun. She felt O'Brien taking hold of her left hand and examining it, and wailed something about his being too late, that she was already dying.

Paying her no mind, he held her bloody hand to his mouth and sucked, feeling the warm, metallic taste of the wound flooding across his tongue. Turning his head to one side, he spat the mixture of blood and venom into the dirt, then repeated the procedure again and again.

His lips felt tender from the coffee she'd thrown at him. The whole of his face felt raw, come to that, and his eyes were still smarting. But his injuries were as nothing compared to hers.

Again he spat out the nauseous blend of blood and poison. The two holes made by the rattler's fangs were inflamed and swollen at the edges. He sucked more blood from them, spat it out, sucked once again. Only when the blood still oozing from them appeared unsullied by stringy trails of transparent toxin did he quit.

By then she'd fallen into a doze, maybe worse, and he pushed himself away from her, went and rinsed his mouth as thoroughly as he could down by the stream.

He emptied the coffee pot, refilled it, stoked up the small fire and set the fresh water to heat through. As he went back over to the girl he cursed his sense of altruism. Had it not been for his belief in justice, he'd never have taken this job on. But take it on he had – and made one hell of a mess of it, too.

He looked down at Maria. Her lips twitched in a series of odd, disjointed mutterings. She looked pale, and her eyelids fluttered in time with her nightmares.

If she died...

Bending, he scooped her up and carried her carefully back to their temporary campsite. He set her down beneath the questionable shade of some mesquite yucca and saltbush, dug out his blanket and draped it across her.

The water began to bubble and he lifted the pot from the flames. Butterflies began to skitter through the warming air as he mixed in some cold, then set about bathing and binding her hand.

Again he glanced at her ashen face. She was young. She was beautiful. Maybe she was going to die.

His sigh came out heavy and tortured.

All he could do now was wait. And hope.

She started threshing around after a while,

once her body started fighting whatever amount of venom was still in her, and great beads of sweat started popping on her forehead. She frowned, she sobbed, she made strange mewing sounds like a cat. Then she fell silent, and something inside him, some pessimistic sense of dread, told him that she was dead.

He grabbed her good hand, felt for a pulse, exhaled when he found one. She was still alive, thank God. But only just. Her breathing was shallow now, the beat of her heart feeble.

It could still go either way.

While her skin grew increasingly hot, he went and unsaddled the animals. It looked like they were going to be here for some time, so he might as well make them comfortable.

His stomach growled, reminding him that he'd had nothing to eat since that can of peaches sixteen hours earlier. He dug into his possibles, found an airtight of beans he'd bought in Little Mesa, opened it and set it among the embers.

As the beans began to warm up, O'Brien examined the girl. Her teeth ground together as violent tremors racked her body. He put a hand to her forehead and felt the heat belching out of her even before their skins touched. Sweat coursed down her face, matting her hair.

He ate the beans with little real appetite, just to stop his stomach rolling, then scanned the terrain around them. The day was hotting up now, and they were out in the middle of nowhere, exposed to its pitiless rays. He had nothing with which to rig up a shelter, and he couldn't risk moving the girl yet. There was nothing for it but to sit it out, occasionally forcing water down the girl to stop her from dehydrating.

The morning wore on.

After the fever, Maria was taken with severe chills. Her temperature dropped rapidly, her face blanched still further, her teeth chattered like castanets and once or twice her glazed eyes opened but remained unseeing. O'Brien piled his wolfskin jacket onto her, the horses' blankets too, and held her down until the shivers stopped. After that, Maria seemed to fall into something more like real slumber, and he went back to his place on the other side of the embers, to await whatever happened next.

By the time noon lay an hour behind them, the heat was almost intolerable. Just sitting in it was enough to knock a man sideways. Wiping sweat from his face, O'Brien decided that a wash and shave might liven him up. He went down to the stream-bank and slowly scraped the salt-and-pepper beard from his jaw.

He was still unable to shake off the feeling of lethargy the heat, combined with his lack of sleep, had induced. For a while he dozed there on the stream-bank, and that was how he got through the afternoon.

Later on the heat began to ease up as the sun sank regally in the west. Maria continued to sleep while O'Brien wiped her face and checked her pulse. For the first time that day he began to feel optimistic about the girl's chances.

She slept peacefully all through the following day, but the sleep was deep and coma-like. O'Brien kept an eye on their surroundings, once he saw a wagon trundling across the flatlands half a mile to the west, but that was all.

By dawn of the third day, Maria was well enough to talk, though still weak.

'*Gracias,*' she said as he lifted her head and held a mug of coffee to her dry, cracked lips. 'I ... I will be better now, yes?'

He studied her through the soft, phosphorescent glow of dawn. She was still pale.

126

Even her full lips were bloodless, and her eyes were ringed with grey loops. 'You should be,' he replied gently.

The news didn't seem to cheer her overmuch. 'If only God had taken me,' she lamented grimly. 'Then you could not have used me to trap my Angel.'

O'Brien took his hand out from under her when he was sure she would be able to sit up on her own. 'Don't think I want to do it this way, Maria,' he said, picking up his own mug. 'I'll tell you straight – I'd as soon face Angel head-on and trust to Providence. But one against so many...'

She stared moodily into her mug, seeing pictures in the rising steam. 'You're wrong about my Angel,' she said.

'So you keep telling me.'

'I have to; because you can't see for yourself that you're being manipulated.'

That was an odd word to use. It made him look down at her sharply. 'Manipulated? Who by?'

Her eyes dropped away from him. 'I don't know,' she admitted reluctantly. 'The Government, perhaps.'

He shrugged. 'Well, the Government – yours as well as mine – sure wants Angel dead, all right. And from all I've heard, with good reason, too.'

'There, you see!' she said earnestly. 'You *hear* that my Angel is this murdering madman you've come to kill, but you don't know it for a *fact*, do you?' Her already weak voice grew even more hoarse, and he realized she was crying. *'Please*, Carter … please, I *beg* you! Spare my Angel, for the love of God!'

'The way he spared his own father, you mean? Or the sister he raped?'

Surprise showed plain on her face. *'What?'*

'You heard,' he said, relenting a little. 'Or maybe you didn't know about that?'

'You're lying,' she said with firm conviction, shaking her head slowly from side to side. Her expression was one of pity, mixed with disgust; it made him feel more uncomfortable than he could have imagined. 'If you kill my Angel,' she warned bleakly, 'you kill a saint.'

Abruptly he tossed the contents of his own mug on the fire and stood up. 'Come on,' he said, squinting out across the savannah to the north. 'We've wasted enough time here. I'll fix up some breakfast, then we'll move out.'

'I can't,' she hedged. 'I'm still too weak.'

His face was grim as he peered down at

her. 'If you're well enough to hate me,' he said soberly. 'I figure you're fit enough to ride.'

For all his tough talk, however, O'Brien was mindful of the girl's weakened condition, and kept their pace comfortably slow. For most of the journey she dozed in her side-saddle, and he watched her carefully, ready to reach across and support her should she suddenly slump. She didn't, though, and as the morning wore on, so the land began to lift towards the towering granite peaks ahead.

They reached *Picar Cumbre* around mid-afternoon. O'Brien knew the spot well from countless previous trips into Mexico. The spire of rock that gave the place its name rose some eighty feet into the muggy air and ended in a point sharpened by the elements. Just beyond it rose a cliff-face into which were set a series of natural shelves. A green cactus garden had grown up there, saguaro, barrel and garambullo, even some gaily-coloured salt-cedar bushes. Rocks littered the hard-packed ground, and the echoes of the newcomers' horse-hooves clattered back at them from the mountains reaching up ahead.

Here some blind prickly pear grew from a crevice in the weathered grey rock-face, there lay the evidence of a recent rock-slide, limestone boulders scattered like a child's playthings across the tan-coloured earth. A jumble of broken *carrizo* reeds surrounded a shallow pool of water some sixty yards to the west.

There was only one way to approach Needle Peak, and that was the way O'Brien and Maria came at it – from the north. To all other points of the compass, the steep, shaly mountains were practically impassable. A man up in among those cactus-thick shelves of rock had a good view of the flatlands to the north, and had little to fear from behind or to either side.

In all, it was a good spot from which to make a kill – as O'Brien found out when someone already up there fired a rifle and blew him out of his saddle.

He was lucky.

The shimmer of the super-heated air must have thrown the rifleman's aim just enough to make his bullet slash O'Brien's left shoulder instead of punch his heart out through his spine.

But there was no time to thank fate as

O'Brien hit the rocky trail with enough force to push the wind out of him; just time to hear Maria scream and fight to control her nervous colt; to roll and pull his .38 from leather; to catch the darting flash of sun on Winchester barrel about sixty feet up the cliff-face and return fire.

The handgun's high-pitched echo cracked across the trapped, sweaty air of Needle Peak. O'Brien followed it with another, then a third. After that he crabbed sideways, behind the cover of a fallen boulder, just as the rifleman began to retaliate.

The Winchester boomed like a cannon. The slug ripped chips out of the other side of the large grey rock. O'Brien waited a moment, cursing the fire in his left shoulder as he tried to gauge the speed with which the rifleman could pump another .44/40 into his weapon.

Four seconds later the long gun boomed again, and the bullet sizzled through the still desert air to kick up a shower of dust six feet away.

O'Brien came around the boulder, crouched, focused on the spot at which he'd last seen his attacker and fired his Colt twice, double-handed.

He heard a yell of alarm spill down from

in among the cacti.

In an instant he was back behind the boulder, reloading the empty handgun as he listened for more tell-tale sounds. All he heard now was the clatter of Maria's horse carrying her to the relative safety of the rocks over by the pool.

A second passed. Blood wormed a stop-start course down his arm. Then another rifle-blast shook the air. More splinters of rock sprayed across him. He stayed where he was, regaining his breath and trying to make sense of this new turn of events.

Another shot crashed out. Two more. But by then O'Brien had bellied down in imitation of the black-tailed rattler he'd killed three days before, and was following a line of low, smooth boulders east across the hot, hard dirt to reach a better vantage-point.

He heard the skittering of disturbed rocks coming from someplace behind him and froze. Sounded like someone coming down the western slope to get him. Twisting onto his side, he chanced a look over the low rocks, saw nothing, no-one.

Again the rifleman up there triggered a shot at the boulder now thirty feet behind him. O'Brien squinted, discerned the dark, blued barrel projecting clearly from all the foliage.

He brought the Colt up and fired, twice.

The rifleman made a wet, gurgly sound of shock. The brightly-coloured bushes up there shivered. Then O'Brien's would-be assassin fell forward, through the screen of greenery, and somersaulted lazily through the air to smash himself among the boulders at the base of the cliff.

In the instant before the man became mush, O'Brien saw a bald head, a thick black beard, recognized the Salazar supporter Elvira had called Alfonso Sanchez.

In that moment he thought he understood everything; that Alfonso, learning of his intentions from Elvira, had decided to beat him to Needle Peak, exact revenge for the humiliation O'Brien had heaped on him, and gain the Angel's favour by rescuing his woman.

Before he had a chance to consider anything else, however, O'Brien heard Maria yelling something in Spanish, and caught the soft sounds of more rocks and loose, pebbly earth skittering down a slope somewhere close by. Tensing, he began a quick but careful scan of the terrain around him.

That was when the kid with the smouldering black eyes and duds to match – Fortino, his name was – loosed a yell and leapt at

133

him from behind.

The kid had a lot of hate in him. That much was obvious from the frown puckering his otherwise smooth Latin features and the fire dancing in his dark eyes. His mouth was wrenched down at the corners as he spewed a stream of Spanish swear-words. He came at O'Brien with his lard-bellied partner's machete in his hand.

O'Brien rolled to one side just before the blade sliced into the ground with a metallic clang. Fortino tore the blade free and tried again. He was fast and he was determined, but since O'Brien had no particular desire to part company with anything God had given him at birth, he had the best reason in the world to be faster and more determined still.

He rolled again, managed to get his feet under him, leapt back, over the line of low boulders and stabbed his double-action Colt at the murderous young Mexican.

'That's far enough, Fortino!' he yelled in Spanish, 'No closer, or I'll shoot!'

Fortino heard him, but his blood was up and he was damned if he'd back down now. He came at O'Brien and O'Brien shot him like he said he would, but because he had no special desire to kill, he aimed low and sent a bullet into the meaty part of the kid's left leg.

Fortino's face screwed up and he screamed like a banshee. Then he crumpled and the machete fell from his grasp as he clutched the leaking wound with both hands.

O'Brien backed away from him, turning to meet any more challengers who might fancy their chances. But Needle Peak was quiet again now, and empty but for Maria and the third member of the trio, Emilio, the lard-bellied, hook-nosed, sombrero-wearing bean-eater whose arm O'Brien had broken just over a week earlier.

Both the man and the girl were standing over by the reed-circled pool, holding guns on him. From where he was standing, it looked to O'Brien as if their reflections had grown out of the soles of their sandals.

'*Bastard!*' Emilio spat, the Merwin and Hulbert in his good hand trembling a little in his rage. 'You'll die this time!'

But even as O'Brien prepared to shoot it out with the last member of the trio, he heard thunder rumbling ominously in the distance.

No, not thunder.

Hoofbeats.

Slowly a heavy sense of dread began to

135

sink down to the pit of his stomach as he turned cautiously to face the newcomers galloping up to the scene in a cloud of dust.

Unless he was very, very mistaken, this would be Angel Salazar and his eight-strong gang of cut-throats.

They looked like a mean pack of bastards.

O'Brien ran grim eyes across them as they reined in thirty feet ahead of him, strung out in a loose, dusty line. He saw tall men, short ones, men with round faces, long faces, be-whiskered and clean-shaven. Their ages ranged from twenty-five to forty. About six of them were Mexican, the other two American. Each of them returned his stare with either open hostility or complete indifference.

Finally he shifted his eye-line towards the man who had reined in his fine chestnut stallion a little ahead of the others, and when their eyes locked, time stopped and everyone else assembled there at Needle Peak simply ceased to exist.

For the leader of this pack of wolves was indeed Angel Salazar.

O'Brien remembered the face of the boy in the daguerreotype Rosalia had given him back in Del Rio. Round, angelic, with dark eyes well-spaced above a long nose and flared nostrils. He looked handsome and assured, almost dangerously charismatic.

Then the rest of the world crowded in on O'Brien once again; he felt the oven-heat against his skin, the harsh glare of the sun, heard flies buzzing, horses shifting, the black-eyed kid, Fortino, moaning. He knew he didn't stand a chance against so many. He knew his life expectancy could be measured in minutes now, maybe even *one* minute.

So he decided, quite coolly, that if he was going to die, then he was going to take the Angel along with him.

With great deliberation he brought his Colt up to line on the bandit leader's heart. Angel met his gaze with narrowed eyes. He was around the mid-twenties, tall from the looks of him, and slim in his sky-blue cotton shirt and tight, flared *vaquero's* pants.

O'Brien extended the handgun to arm's length in the classic shootist's posture. From the edge of his vision he saw the Angel's men reaching for their own weapons.

He looked directly into Angel's eyes and heard in his mind fragments of all that Maria had said in the last couple of days.

You're wrong about my Angel, she'd said.

You hear that he's this murdering madman you've come to kill, but you don't know it for a fact.

Seconds ticked by.

If you kill my Angel, she'd said, *you kill a saint.*

And something else too.

You can't see that you're being manipulated. Manipulated.

O'Brien knew an instant of doubt. It was crazy, sure; but what if she was right? Almost before he realized it, he slowly lowered his right arm back to his side, and thought he saw the Angel's broad shoulders relax a little with a sigh.

'Drop the gun,' the bandit said quietly, in English.

For better or worse, O'Brien did just that.

'Now,' said Angel Salazar, reverting to Spanish and motioning to a couple of the men to his left. 'Take him and tie him tight and stow him over by the pool. He interests me, this *gringo;* I don't know what to make of him yet. But I will, *senor.* And when I do – that's when you'll die.'

SEVEN

The two men Angel had indicated dismounted, grabbed a length of hemp and hustled over to their captive. O'Brien allowed them to twist him around and tie his hands behind his back without protest, although he started to think that maybe he'd made a mistake in not killing Angel while he had the chance.

While the two bandits busied themselves tying an intricate and escape-proof series of knots, he watched Emilio help the still-weak Maria across to her lover. When she was near enough, Angel came down out of his saddle and scooped her up into his arms. For a moment both their faces were transformed as they held each other. Then, because he'd seen how pale she still looked, and noticed the crude bandage on her left hand, Angel held her at arm's length and began to question her worriedly.

'There,' said one of the bandits behind O'Brien, 'That should hold you. Now, off you go, *gringo;* over to the pool.'

A shove in the back got him moving.

By the time he'd made it over to the shallow tank of water and flopped down among the *carrizo* reeds, another of Angel's men had started to fashion a rope corral for the horses, his own included; another set about examining the bullet-wound in Fortino's leg; two more dragged the late Alfonso Sanchez out from the rocks at the base of the cliff and carried him off, presumably, for burial.

Within the quarter-hour coffee was bubbling, guards had been posted up among the rockshelves, the remainder were taking their ease and the Angel was talking in earnest to the beautiful Maria, while Emilio, his right arm still in a sling, stared across at O'Brien with hatred plain in his sombrero-shaded eyes.

After a while O'Brien had seen enough, and turned his attention to his bullet-creased left shoulder. It hurt like a bitch now, thanks to the less-than-kind treatment he'd suffered at the hands of the men who'd tied him. But he didn't think the wound was so bad. At least the bleeding had stopped. All he had to worry about now was whether or not there'd be any more pain still to come.

As the afternoon wore on the sky grew a dirty, smoke-coloured grey. The men amused themselves with cards or dice, drank coffee and ate meagre rations. Along about five o'clock, Angel, Maria and Emilio came over to O'Brien and stared down at him with expressions difficult to read.

A moment passed, until Emilio glanced across at his leader. Angel met his eyes and nodded.

Using his good hand, Emilio drew his machete.

O'Brien clenched his teeth. So – the time had come, then. He glared up at his captors, damned if he'd show them any of the fear squeezing at his innards. Angel met his eyes and smiled; Maria, too, stared down at him with her lips slightly parted. In the background, the Angel's men watched with interest as Emilio went around behind O'Brien and raised the machete high above his head, then brought it down.

But before O'Brien could flinch or cry out, a new fact suddenly registered in his mind.

Emilio wasn't using the blade to kill him, but rather to saw through the ropes binding his hands.

It was the work of a moment to slice

through them. Thirty seconds later, O'Brien was massaging his wrists to bring life back to his stiff arms, and wondering just what in hell the Angel was playing at.

'Coffee, *gringo?*' the bandit leader asked in a soft, cultured voice.

O'Brien eyed him carefully, betraying none of his surprise, then said, 'Sure.'

Angel said something to Maria and she turned and went back to the small camp-fire to fetch him a cup. The bandit watched her go for a moment, then hunkered down on the far side of the pool to study O'Brien closely.

The man O'Brien had come south to kill had a smooth skin the colour of milky coffee. He had taken off his sombrero to reveal thick black hair slicked flat to his skull. He said, 'By rights, I should have had you killed the moment we rode in.'

O'Brien kept his expression neutral. 'But you didn't.'

'No. I was curious to see this man who presumed to kidnap *mi amiga* and lure me to my death.'

Maria came back and handed O'Brien a steaming mug. He took it, nodded his thanks and returned his gaze to Angel. 'Well,' he said. 'You've seen me. What happens now?'

Angel's smile was genuine, and actually quite engaging, which only served to make O'Brien even more curious. After all, he'd expected to find some sort of slobbering, hair-trigger lunatic, but here was someone entirely different. 'Such courage in the face of death,' the bandit muttered.

O'Brien took a sip of coffee, waiting for him to get to the point. He didn't have to wait long.

'It might interest you to know that three things have stopped me from ordering your execution, O'Brien,' the Angel said sociably. 'One is that you are obviously no friend of the Mexican authorities, having had to fight your way out of Piedras Negras with a detachment of *rurales* on your tail. Another is that my *querida* here tells me that you saved her life when she was bitten by a snake, which naturally puts me in your debt.'

O'Brien tried to shrug, but with a shoulder crusted with so much dried blood, it wasn't easy. 'And the third thing?' he pressed.

'Something Maria here tells me you said to her earlier on.' Angel paused deliberately, so that he could watch O'Brien's reaction closely when he finally revealed what it was. 'Something,' he said, 'about my father and my sister.'

143

O'Brien remained poker-faced, 'What about them?'

'I'm curious. Who told you that I raped my sister? And just what am I supposed to have done to my father?'

O'Brien smiled with his mouth only. 'You mean to say it just slipped your mind?'

'Tell me, *hombre!*' Angel prodded. 'There's no official price on my head yet, so far as I know. So who told you these lies and paid you to kill me?' Before O'Brien could reply, however, the bandit muttered a name. 'Molina!' he hissed. 'Of course! That would explain it.' He eyed O'Brien shrewdly. 'Who was it – an uncle, perhaps? My father, even?'

O'Brien kept quiet.

'Is that why you undertook this *loco* plan to kill me?' Angel asked, his voice growing softer and more sibilant. 'Because that cripple talked you into saving the honour of the family name?'

There was no point in denying it, so O'Brien said, 'Yes.'

Angel laughed. He threw back his head and let loose a loud chuckle that set his Adam's apple bouncing. But the laughter was grim, and when he looked at O'Brien again, his face was deadly serious.

'That explains it, then,' he said quietly.

'You know, I'm glad I didn't have you killed, O'Brien. Because, as it turns out, I have no quarrel with you. Whatever you did to engineer this meeting, you did because you thought it was right, which makes you blameless, just a pawn in a much larger game.'

O'Brien frowned, now thoroughly mystified. 'What's that supposed to mean?'

'That you've been *had*, O'Brien. Duped. Fooled.' Angel showed his even teeth in a sad smile. *'Manipulated,'* he said.

Sitting there among the *carrizo* reeds with his left arm hurting like hell, O'Brien tried to make sense of Angel's words, but couldn't. A moment passed, then he said, 'I don't understand?'

'It's quite simple,' Angel replied grimly. 'The man who claimed to be my father or uncle or whatever – and I know exactly who he is, *senor* – is an impostor. My beloved father has been dead these last eight months, God rest him. And as for my sister…'

Something unpleasant was starting to grow in O'Brien's belly. 'Yes?'

'I haven't *got* one,' Angel said with a shrug. 'I was an only child.'

'I've heard of you, O'Brien.' Angel's voice

had taken on a gentler, calmer tone. 'They say you are a man of honour. I certainly hope so.'

The bandit leader reached behind him, withdrew O'Brien's Colt from where it had been tucked into his own weapons-belt and held it out. 'Here,' he said. 'I return this to you as a gesture of goodwill. To convince you of my sincerity. Take it.'

O'Brien held back a moment, licking his lips. He looked beyond Angel, and the rough-and-tumble crew scattered around Needle Peak, expecting a trick. His eyes flicked up to Maria, standing proudly beside her lover. She nodded. He reached out and took the .38, checking it to satisfy himself that it was in working order. Carefully, so as not to spook anyone into doing anything rash, he thumbed five fresh rounds from his belt and reloaded the weapon.

'Now,' said Angel, 'I think perhaps we should try to make sense of this business, don't you? We'd better take a look at that shoulder of yours, too.'

O'Brien slipped the Colt back into leather. Its weight seemed to give him renewed strength. 'Thanks.'

It was funny how things sometimes turned out, he thought. Not so long before, he'd had

146

to patch Maria up. Now, as the men went back to their cards and dice and Emilio stamped off to join them, it became Maria's job to fix *his* wound.

Stripping to the waist, O'Brien allowed her to bathe the shallow but crusty crease. He still wasn't thoroughly convinced that Angel Salazar was the benign figure he liked to present, but maybe his opinion might change by the time they'd tried to straighten everything out.

'So,' said the bandit, once O'Brien had told him pretty much what had happened down in the Texas Ranger barracks at Del Rio. 'That is their latest attempt to discredit me among my followers, is it? By spreading the story that I crippled my own father and raped my sister.' He snorted his contempt. 'I'd have thought they could have done better than that.'

'Who's "they"?' asked O'Brien.

Angel met his intense gaze and held it without looking away. 'The Mexican Government,' he replied. Seeing O'Brien's frown deepen, he said, 'Perhaps it will become clearer once I explain that I – *we* – are not the thieves and killers the Government, or my so-called "father", would have you believe. Oh, we rob and we kill, when we have to, certainly. But the innocent are never our targets. Indeed, it is the innocent of this country that we have formed ourselves to represent.'

'You're revolutionaries,' O'Brien guessed.

'*Si*. Bitterly opposed to the tyranny of Porfirio Diaz and his puppet president, Manuel Gonzalez,' Angel admitted with feeling. He watched Maria rub salve gently on O'Brien's raw shoulder-wound. 'I'm not sure how much you know about the politics of my country,' he said. 'They're so complex, I doubt if I could simplify them for you. But I will try.'

As Maria bound his arm, O'Brien listened to Angel and began to face the fact that he had indeed been duped. As he spoke of his beloved country, O'Brien realized that in no way was Angel the kill-crazy madman he'd been led to believe. He was rational, balanced, clear in both thought and speech.

Briefly he charted Porfirio Diaz' rise to power back in 1876, when he had ousted his main political opponent, Dr Lerdo de Tejada, by inciting revolution.

Diaz, a Spanish-Indian half-breed, apparently had much ambition and few scruples. Once the Presidency was his, he began to rule Mexico with an iron hand. Although a

dictator well-known for his swift and sometimes bloody retaliation against anyone who
dared to defy the policies of his regime,
however, there could be no denying that he
had brought prosperity back to his country's
ailing economy. But that prosperity was not
without price.

'We have seen growth in our banks, our
railroads and ports, and foreign investors
have seen fit to sink much-needed funds into
our many industries, it is true,' Angel
continued. 'But what have all these advance-
ments brought to the lowly *peones?* Nothing,
O'Brien. Look at this land. Precious little
has been invested in *that.* Farming has been
almost totally neglected, and poverty is
widespread. The Indians, and those of the
working classes, are ill-treated and poorly-
housed. While they starve and live in fear of
the armed forces, who ride roughshod over
them whenever they can, the ruling class live
like kings.'

In 1880, he said, Diaz had been forced to
relinquish his Presidency because an
amendment in his country's Constitution
forbade him from campaigning for a second
term of office. To get around this, he had
allowed the title to pass on to his close but
largely ineffective ally, Manuel Gonzalez; so,

149

in effect, Diaz still ruled.

'Already he is making moves to amend our Constitution once more,' Angel explained. 'So that it will be possible for him to run for office again in the coming election. He'll get what he wants, too; he's that powerful.

'Meanwhile, the masses grow poorer under his rule, and more prone to abuse. Someone must stand up to him, show him that he cannot intimidate everyone.'

'And that someone is you?'

Angel shrugged. '*Sí.* And my father before me – until he grew too vocal in his criticism and Diaz had some of his underlings arrange an "accident" for him.'

O'Brien frowned. 'Your father was a politician?'

'After a fashion. A financier, until my mother died. After that he neglected commerce and began to involve himself in the hardships faced by the proletariat.'

Shrugging slowly back into his shirt, O'Brien digested all that he had heard. Finally, he said, 'So all of this business up in Del Rio with the man who claimed to be your father was just a charade; a way of persuading me to kill you?'

Angel nodded, the twist of his lips signifying his disgust. 'Just after my father was murdered,' he said, 'I began to travel around the country, speaking to the masses in much the same way as he had. Nobody listened, of course. I was considered too young to know much of worth or wisdom, so the Government paid me no mind.

'Then, slowly, the *peones* began to take notice of what I had to say. I spoke until I was hoarse, and the volume of support I had gained could not easily be measured. *That* is when I came under the scrutiny of the Government, O'Brien. When I became a threat.'

His smile turned bleak. 'I was speaking in Matamoro, perhaps five or six months ago, when a Government lackey made an attempt on my life. I was lucky. My would-be killer was not. When the crowd caught up with him, they literally tore him apart.

'After that, my support virtually doubled overnight. But I was forced into hiding for a time. Whenever I could, I continued to spread the word of my people. I tried to give them back their pride, their dignity; tried to convince them the way of things in this country *could* change if only they stood firm.

'But always I had to move on, for Diaz saw me as a very real danger now. Eventually I left all the trappings of my previous life behind me and became, to all intents and purposes, a bandit.

'I think it was this "bandit" idea that inspired the Government to attempt to discredit me. A number of Government troops, masquerading as my men and I, committed several outrages up along the border in an attempt to disillusion my followers.'

'That would be the series of crimes Captain Taylor told me about,' O'Brien cut in. 'The rapes, murders and stagecoach robberies.'

'Most of them, yes,' Angel agreed. 'But there were *some* crimes which could not be so easily blamed on others.'

O'Brien's frown asked the question. Maria answered it.

'The men you see here today,' she said, speaking for the first time in half an hour, 'they are good men. Men who believe in our cause, and who are loyal beyond question to my Angel. But there were others, some months ago, who came to join us in the mistaken belief that Angel really *was* a bandit.'

'There were four of them,' Angel continued. 'All Americans. One night they abused the hospitality of some of my friends up in Puerto Madero. Robbed them, raped their daughters, then rode north and killed two men whilst robbing a bank in Texas.' He faced O'Brien directly. 'That very nearly *did* ruin me in the eyes of my followers, as you can imagine. That's why I too rode north – to find them, bring them back and punish them.'

O'Brien could guess what form the punishment had taken; a bullet in the guts or a noose around the neck. Staring off across the slowly darkening landscape, he remembered something Maria had said that murky midnight in Piedras Negras, when he'd abducted her. 'Some of his men,' she'd remarked, 'it was a mistake to have ever taken them on.'

'Of course,' Angel went on, 'the Government has continued in its attempts to assassinate me or my character. But in trying to recruit so famous a fighting-man as yourself to kill me, they've shown just how big a threat to them I really *have* become.'

O'Brien nodded, but said nothing. He was thinking about the beating he'd taken in the alleyway that first night in Piedras Negras; his escape from Major Iniestra's men; how he'd intimidated and pistol-whipped Emilio and the others in order to locate the Angel; and finally, how he'd been forced to kill Alfonso Sanchez, and wound the kid, Fortino.

All of it, he thought angrily, because a bunch of worthless politicians had chosen to *manipulate* him.

'This man,' he said. 'The one who claimed to be your father. Who is he?'

'Jacinto Molina,' Angel replied. 'No relation at all, though he was once considered a family friend. He was quite well-known here at one time, an actor – Shakespeare, Federico, that kind of thing. Then he had an accident, fell through a faulty trap-door on stage one night and broke both his legs. About a year later he suffered a stroke and retired from public life. He had long been a supporter of Diaz and his policies. He and my father used to argue them passionately, I remember. Then, one evening, all the rhetoric turned to insults, the insults finally to blows. Molina left our house and never returned.'

Angel grew quiet for a moment, temporarily lost in the past. Then he said, 'I have quite a network of informants, O'Brien, and word of anything unusual that they believe I should know about always finds its way to me.

'That Jacinto Molina was summoned to Mexico City on some matter concerning me filtered down through that network a few months ago. At first I could make no sense of it. After all, I had not seen him for years. Then I received word that Molina and his daughter had been dispatched to the United States on some unspecified errand.

'Then I was truly mystified; even more so when another of my supporters, who has access to such information, told me that a large sum of money had been paid into Molina's Chiralita City bank account.

'That he had been hired for – and then sent *upon* – some kind of secret mission was obvious. But what was it? And how did it concern me?

'Now, of course, it all makes sense. By fooling the American authorities with another of his winning performances, Molina was able to engage *your* services, O'Brien. And in recruiting a *Yanqui* to kill me, the Mexican Government neatly distanced itself still further from my murder.'

O'Brien sighed. 'So,' he said after a while. 'What happens now? You've been straight with me, Angel, as I hope I've been with you. Can you trust me to ride on back to the States now, and take care of your "father"?'

Angel nodded. 'I believe so. But will you not be riding with us for a day or two? There is some business we have to take care of several miles to the west that I believe will appeal to you.'

O'Brien shook his head. He felt tired, but more than that, hungry to settle his score in Del Rio. 'If it's all the same to you, I'll be riding north come sun-up.'

'As you will,' Angel said. 'I just thought you might enjoy striking back at the Government after what two of their *colorados* did to your friend.'

O'Brien glanced at him sharply. 'What? What's that you said?'

Angel frowned at him. 'You mean you didn't *know*? This man you were with ... Emilio! What did you say that *hombre* was called?'

Emilio, sitting a few yards away, looked up from a dog-eared hand of cards. 'Morgan,' he supplied.

Angel nodded. 'That's right; Morgan–'

O'Brien got a picture of the big, guileless cowboy he'd met in Piedras Negras. He saw Shep Morgan's big, solid bulk, his oblong face and squinting eyes. Most of all, however, he remembered the man's many kindnesses to him, and the fact that he hadn't been able to repay even one.

'What about him?' he asked through gritted teeth.

Angel said, 'Evidently, two *colorados* summoned to Piedras Negras by your friend Major Iniestra had him dragged in for questioning. According to Emilio, they were convinced the two of you were in cahoots.'

O'Brien felt his scarred fists folding into dangerous weapons but made no move to relax them. 'What did they do to him?' he demanded.

'What they do with all their prisoners,' Angel replied. 'Systematically beat him until they were finally satisfied that he knew nothing of value about you.'

O'Brien got up fast, making Maria jump a little, and gasp. For a moment all he wanted to do was grab his horse and head back to Piedras Negras. Then the calm, reasoning part of his mind reasserted itself and he forced himself to simmer down. 'How bad did they hurt him?'

'The way Emilio tells it, a couple of broken ribs, a fractured jaw, one or two broken fingers, possibly a broken nose.'

As the catalogue of horrors unwound, O'Brien felt himself growing colder and calmer and ever more calculating. The rage left him, but not the burning lust for revenge. He stared out into the closing darkness. 'Where is he now?' he asked in a strange, flat voice.

'The *colorados* released him into the care of a local doctor, Ramirez. He was doctored and sent home.'

'Damn.'

'He'll be all right,' Angel said, coming closer to put a hand on his shoulder. 'Given time. But–'

'Who were they?' O'Brien cut in. 'These *colorados?*'

'Two heartless barbarians well-known to us, Colonel Manuel Redarte and a snake in man's skin by the name of Raul Gerardo, who holds the rank of captain.'

'I want them, Angel.'

Angel squeezed his shoulder in understanding. 'I know, *mi amigo*. But they left Piedras Negras as soon as they realized they'd get nothing further from your friend. They're probably halfway back to Mexico City by now.'

O'Brien swore under his breath, still looking out across the lonely, night-shrouded savannah. Again he thought of the man who'd claimed to be Angel's father. This business with Shep was yet another consequence of Jacinto Molina's deceit. Finally he turned to see Angel and Maria regarding him with concern.

158

'All right,' he said. 'You say you've got some business to the west, a way to strike back at the Government. Count me in. But only if we can stop by a town that's on the telegraph line.'

'We can do that easily enough,' Angel replied cautiously. 'But why? You want to send a message to someone, obviously. But *who?*'

O' Brien said, 'Colonel Redarte. I want to get the sonofabitch back here as soon as I can; and then I'm going to make him pay, Angel. So help me, I'm going to make him *pay.*'

At first light the following morning O'Brien and the others broke camp, ate a quick breakfast of biscuits and beans, saddled up and prepared to head west.

'Maria's coming with us?' O'Brien asked when it became obvious that she would not be accompanying Emilio and Fortino back to Piedras Negras.

Angel Salazar ran one smooth palm along his chestnut stallion's glistening neck as he nodded. 'Maria's coming with us,' he confirmed. 'For it is a sad but true fact that gossip spreads, O'Brien, and it is almost certain that word of her kidnap will eventually

159

reach the ears of the *rurales;* that, and the reason *why* she was kidnapped.' He looked sad, but his tone carried no malice towards O'Brien. 'For Maria to return to Piedras Negras ever again is out of the question. As soon as the authorities learned of our relationship, they would use her as a lever against me just as quickly as you did. But don't look so miserable, my friend. It could be worse. As it is, we can set Maria up somewhere else, perhaps change her name.'

'It's still a hell of a thing, though,' O'Brien said. 'She had folks in that town.' He paused a moment. 'I really *am* sorry, Angel.'

'I know. But enough talk. Let's ride, *mi hermanos!*'

The small group left Needle Peak while the air was still cool, trending north. After about a mile, they broke apart. The bulk of the riders cut away to the western flatlands; Emilio and the roughly-doctored Fortino cantered back to Piedras Negras.

Sometime around eleven o'clock one of the scouts Angel had sent out ahead came back to the main column to report that a small detachment of rural police were crossing the wasteland about half a mile directly ahead.

Angel considered that. Then he told the

scout to go back and keep an eye on them until they'd left the area, and directed the rest of his men down into the cover of a dusty, twisting arroyo until the coast was clear.

It was once they'd all dismounted and seen to the comfort of their horses that O'Brien asked the handsome revolutionary about this bit of 'business' he had planned.

Angel's teeth flashed white against his tan. 'Ah,' he said with relish. 'I think you will like it, O'Brien. Come, let's rest our bones, and I'll tell you more.'

Together with Maria, they took their canteens and found a patch of halfway flat ground. Hunkering down beneath the growing sunlight, Angel said, 'You remember yesterday, when I mentioned all the foreign investors Diaz has attracted to our country?'

O'Brien nodded.

'Well, as you might expect, the majority of them are American. They've come out from your eastern cities and simply taken over our mining concerns, our ports, timber trade and – such as it is – our agriculture. In short, they're virtually bleeding us dry.'

'And Diaz is letting them get away with it?'

Angel nodded. 'For a "consideration",' he

said meaningfully.

O'Brien snorted his disgust, then said, 'Go on.'

'One such "consideration" is on its way to Jose Limantour, our Minister of Finance, even as we speak. Ten million pesos! Can you imagine it?'

O'Brien whistled quietly. 'I can imagine the good it could do for all those poor, starving masses you were talking about.'

'Exactly. A platoon of *federales* are transporting it from Guanajo, in the north, to the railroad in Hidalgo del Valles, about seventy, eighty miles to the west.'

'And we're going to take it,' O'Brien guessed.

Angel's smile broadened. '*Si.*'

'You have a plan?'

'We don't really need one. To get from Guanajo to Hidalgo del Valles, the *federales* will have to pass through *Cañon de Sangre*. That is where we will ambush them.'

'And you're sure it will work?'

'The *federales* will be easy meat, believe me. These transactions are normally conducted in utmost secrecy, so the *solados* rarely encounter problems. It was only by chance that I found about *this* little shipment.'

O'Brien nodded his understanding, but

now that he knew what they were going to do, his thoughts turned back to the *colorados*, Redarte and Gerardo. 'About that wire I wanted to send,' he began.

Angel held up one hand, palm out. 'Don't worry. This afternoon we should be within sight of Tanapa. And I have some friends in the telegraph office there who will be *more* than willing to help you bait your trap.'

The Angel was as good as his word, too. Around mid-afternoon they reined in on a ridge overlooking the small, sleepy-looking town of Tanapa. 'There,' the revolutionary said, addressing O'Brien's rugged profile. 'Jorge here will go with you, and square things with my friend the telegrapher.'

O'Brien nodded. 'Thanks.'

Twenty minutes later the two men rejoined their comrades spelling their mounts up on the ridge. 'Any problems?' Angel asked expectantly.

'Not a one,' O'Brien replied, eyeing the revolutionary shrewdly. 'In fact, your friend down there couldn't help me fast enough. Seems Tanapa had some trouble with the *colorados* about a year ago. The bastards took twelve of their young men away one night and shot them on suspicion of treason.'

'That's right,' Angel nodded grimly. 'The

murdering pigs!' Turning his heat-flushed face to the west, he summoned a smile. 'But that is all in the past now. Let's press on to *Cañon de Sangre, mi amigo* – and make sure we get there in good time to give the *federales* a warm and noisy welcome.'

EIGHT

That night, feeling dusty and saddle-sore, they camped well off the main trail and in among a pungent splash of greenery. Angel posted guards and joined the rest of the men in wolfing down a meager supper, then suggested they turn in early. Being too tired to do otherwise, they did. Sometime around mid-morning the following day, however, they finally reached *Cañon de Sangre* – Blood Canyon.

As soon as they walked their horses cautiously into its southernmost entrance, O'Brien saw why the gorge had been so-named. Eons earlier, some geological fluke had dyed the walls stretching skyward to either side of the curving trail a peculiar blend of red and orange.

Nothing moved within the canyon, not even the scantiest of breezes. Only the echoes of their horses' hooves broke the silence. O'Brien took off his hat and wiped his face. He, like all of them, scanned their surroundings carefully, and with a professional fighting-man's eye for detail.

The trail snaking out ahead shimmered in the trapped heat. It was about sixty feet wide in most places, and at least three hundred feet long. The soft, sandy earth was littered with boulders of varying sizes, and sprinkled with clumps of prickly pear and ocotillo. Glancing from left to right, O'Brien ran his transparent blue eyes up and over the seamed, crimson rock-faces, finding a dozen or more places from which Angel's men would be able to fire down on the *federales* in almost complete safety.

Wheel-ruts showed plainly on the ground in front of them, but they were at least a week old, and by Angel's calculations, which in turn were based on information he'd been able to gather from yet more of his 'friends' in Mexico City, the platoon of Government troops transporting Limantour's millions to the railroad were not due through here for at least another twenty-four hours.

O'Brien watched Angel dismount and stretch his back. The revolutionary looked tired, for he had taken a lengthy turn at guard-duty himself the previous night, but he did not allow himself the luxury of relaxing for long. Turning to study his men, among whom O'Brien was bunched, he said, 'Jorge; you and Grady ride out to the far end of the canyon. Find yourselves good vantage-points with plenty of cover, and keep a lookout for any sign of the *federales*. The moment you spot them, I want you both back here, *comprende?*'

'*Si, jefe!*'

'Luis, you and Esteban will relieve them at sundown.'

'*Si.*'

As Jorge and Grady galloped away, Angel reached up and helped Maria down from her colt. The girl, too, was weary, but just happy enough to be with her lover.

The rest of the men dismounted and began to search for a decent campsite. O'Brien, going with them, allowed his thoughts to turn once again to Shep Morgan, and the telegram he'd sent to the big cowboy's interrogators.

About two hundred kilometers to the south and east of Blood Canyon, Colonel Redarte and his assistant, Captain Gerardo, rode into the town of Frontera nursing saddle-sores of their own.

Although life with the *colorados* had its privileges, chasing *gringo* troublemakers halfway across the country was not one of them, and though they were both fiercely loyal to the Porfirian regime, the colonel and his captain were now looking forward to a return to the easy life in Mexico City.

But Mexico City still lay many kilometers to the south, Colonel Redarte reminded himself, and until they reached the railroad in Hidalgo del Valles, they would have to continue their journey on horseback.

Still, now that they'd finally reached Frontera, at least the *colorados* could cheer themselves with the prospect of feather beds and properly-cooked food. Sleeping on boards or hard, unyielding earth was all well and good for the *peones,* but for the elite it was not only humiliating, but also intensely uncomfortable.

Almost as soon as they'd entered town, word of their presence began to spread. The colonel saw it in the frightened sideways glances he and Gerardo received from the locals as they kept their salt-encrusted horses moving ever closer to the centre of town.

Ah, but Redarte enjoyed the fear his uniform – and in particular, the red band around his peaked cap – inspired. And he knew that Gerardo, whose sadistic tendencies had made him ideal material for the *colorados,* enjoyed it too. Now, the two officers positively bathed in the covert attention their arrival had caused.

Surveying their surroundings through red-rimmed eyes, the officers realized that Frontera's main street was really little more than a wide strip of dirt bordered by two rows of low, sand-coloured *jacales*. Here and there some children played in the shade. Dogs sprawled beneath stunted Joshua trees, while chickens strutted and squabbled in the dust. The afternoon was Hades-hot, and the *colorados* were baking inside their grey-green uniform.

At last Redarte broke the silence between them to raise the hand holding the riding-crop and say, 'There.' He gestured to a cantina that looked to be doing slow, *siesta*-time business. 'We'll try their food and *tequila*, Gerardo. Fortify ourselves against the next leg of our journey, eh?'

Si, coronel,' Gerardo replied with a nod.

They angled their horses towards the *pulqueria*, scattering the chickens before them, each man comfortably aware of the eyes following their every movement from behind dusty, shadowed windows.

The cantina was a simple square building. They dismounted before it, hitched their horses at the tie-rack and entered the place through a creaking front door. The cantina was deserted but for the owner, polishing a glass behind his low bar, and two sleepy-eyed patrons nursing cloudy home-brewed drinks.

When Gerardo closed the door behind them, the owner almost dropped the glass he'd been working on. His dark eyes grew round as he recognized their uniforms and he began to stumble over a greeting.

'Ah ... *senores*... Ah, welcome to my humble–'

'*Tequila*,' Gerardo said imperiously. 'Some food, also.'

The cantina owner bobbed his balding head eagerly, his eyes shuttling from the older man, the *coronel* – he of the long face, hollowed cheeks and strangely blue eyes beneath the heavy white brows – to the tall, thickset *capitan*, whose round, mournful face and heavy-lidded hazel eyes would have looked more fitting on an undertaker.

'But ... but of course, *senores!* Meat-balls? Would meat-balls be acceptable?'

'They will do,' said Gerardo. 'Serve them with beans and rice.'

'*Si, senor!* At once!'

The owner rushed outside by way of an arched doorway off to his right, and a moment later they heard him passing their order on to someone else, most probably his wife.

Taking off their caps and brushing dust from their tunics, the *colorados* claimed a corner table and made themselves comfortable. Some flies were circling the ceiling. They sounded loud in the sudden silence. As if by mutual consent, the two men who'd been drinking up at the bar suddenly set down their glasses and hurriedly made their exit.

After a moment, Gerardo said, 'I'll ask the owner of this place if he can point us towards a decent rooming-house, shall I?'

Redarte nodded. 'Yes, do that.'

As Gerardo got up and strode over to the bar, the colonel's thoughts drifted back over the events of the last week.

That business back in Piedras Negras had turned out to be extremely disappointing, he thought. The man O'Brien had long been wanted by the authorities. That he had actually been held by the *rurales* and then allowed to escape was almost beyond credit. Still, Major Iniestra would pay for his incompetence. The damning report Redarte carried in his satchel would see to that.

Fleetingly, Redarte's mind turned to the

171

other *gringo*, Morgan. He'd been convinced that the man was somehow connected with O'Brien. At first he had even complimented the big fellow on his loyalty, for he had steadfastly refused to disclose anything about O'Brien's whereabouts. But how many men could suffer the broken fingers, the shattered ribs, the dislocated jaw and all the other cuts and bruises and still remain loyal to the fellow who had run off and left him to it?

No, it was regrettable, but Redarte had finally had to concede his mistake. Apparently Morgan *was* innocent, as Iniestra had said. But no matter. Morgan would be patched up and sent home; and should he attempt to make something more of what had happened to him, he would soon find the governments of both their countries infuriating in their slowness and lack of cooperation.

As Gerardo returned to their table, he looked up. 'There is a place further along the street where we might find lodgings for the night,' the captain reported. 'I have the name of the landlady.'

Within twenty minutes their meal had arrived and they slowly began to work their way through it. The food was actually quite good, though it would have pained both

172

officers to have admitted it.

They were just finishing up when a rather corpulent seventy-year-old came in and fixed them with a firm stare. The man was dressed in black pants and a loose white shirt open at the throat. He had a jowly face and loose lips, a swarthy complexion, thinning grey hair and a nose like an onion. In his left hand he held an envelope.

Glancing up at him, Redarte frowned, for unlike his fellow townsmen, this *hombre* showed them no fear, and even less respect. Indeed, his manner was almost blatantly insolent.

He came over to their table and met the colonel's gaze directly '*Buenas dias, senores,*' he said in an age-weakened but still authoritative voice. 'I am Hermano de Sanaja, the head man of Frontera.'

Redarte nodded. Gerardo simply eyed the newcomer with something like distaste. Neither of them asked Sanaja to have a seat, and neither did he presume to take one.

'I bring you this,' he went on, extending the hand holding the envelope. 'Assuming your name is Redarte, colonel.'

'It is!' snapped Redarte, irritated by the other man. He snatched the envelope away from him, ran his blue eyes across it, saw that it was a telegram, and that it had been sealed at the Frontera telegraph office. 'Very good, Sanaja. You may go now.'

The head man gave a little bow, and an insolent smile played at his fleshy lips. 'Thank you,' he said in a tone that made it difficult to judge whether or not he was mocking them. 'Enjoy what remains of your meal, *senores.*'

He turned, waved to the man behind the bar, then let himself back out into the harsh afternoon sunlight. By that time, however, the *colorados* had dismissed him from their minds, and were concentrating on the telegram.

Redarte tore open the envelope and extracted the yellow slip within. Gerardo watched him expectantly. Finally the colonel said, *'Bueno!* They have him, Gerardo, or at least they *think* they do!'

'*Coronel?*'

'Here, see for yourself.'

Redarte gave him the telegram and he scanned it quickly. It had originally been sent to the colonel in Mexico City, but one of their subordinates had wired it back to the towns Redarte and he would have to pass through on their way to Hidalgo del Valles. The wire said:

174

WE ARE HOLDING MAN FITTING
DESCRIPTION OF YOUR SUSPECT
O'BRIEN STOP AWAIT INSTRUC-
TIONS MESSAGE ENDS

It was signed by someone called Xavier
Gonzalez, who was apparently the local
constable of a town called Tanapa.

Gerardo put the wire down and without
waiting to be told, took a much-folded map
from one of his tunic pockets. Shifting their
plates to one side, he unfolded the map and
together the two men studied it.

'Here,' Gerardo said at length,pointing. 'It
gets even better, colonel! That town is
hardly more than a hundred and fifty kilo-
metres away.'

Redarte chuckled. 'Excellent, Gerardo! It
looks as if we didn't have such a wasted trip
after all.'

'If O'Brien *is* the man they're holding.'

'True, true.' Redarte reached up and sig-
nalled for the cantina owner to bring them
more *tequila*. 'But either way, our course is
clear. We will spend the night here in Frontera as planned, but head northwest first
thing in the morning, instead of continuing
on to Hidalgo del Valles.'

175

'*Si, coronel.*'

Gerardo read the telegram one more time. He knew the name of the town from some bother with suspected traitors a year or so back. The name of the constable, however, was unknown to him. Still, what did that matter, so long as the fellow had indeed apprehended the man they were after?

O'Brien, Angel and the others hung around Blood Canyon for the next thirty-six hours, killing time instead of *federales* until a big-bellied American called Grady and Jorge, his slighter, black-haired *compadre*, finally came hightailing it back from their lookout post at the far end of the canyon.

'They're comin'!' Grady reported in reasonable Spanish.

In an instant Angel, Maria and everyone else had gathered around the newcomers. 'You're sure?' Angel demanded.

'Saw 'em plain as day through this here spyglass Angel.'

Angel nodded, his jawline tense. 'How far are they?'

'Maybe half a mile.'

'And how many?'

'Like you heard, a platoon or thereabouts. Fifteen men, no more.'

176

Angel reached out and clapped Grady on the arm. 'Good work, both of you.' Then he spun on his heel to address the others. 'All right, men – to your positions!'

Suddenly their peaceful campsite there in the canyon became a hive of activity as the men started checking their guns and heading for those spots to which Angel had assigned them the previous day. The horses had already been picketed in a well-grassed dip of land up beyond the canyon's western ridge. Now, under orders from her lover, Maria hitched up her somewhat shabby blue dress and began to hustle towards the canyon exit, there to take the trail on her right and head on up to join them.

As O'Brien strode over to the handsome revolutionary, Angel flashed him a brief, tight smile. 'You'll be all right, my friend?' he asked, indicating O'Brien's wounded shoulder.

O'Brien nodded. 'Count on it.'

'Good. Let's make haste, then.'

By the time they'd scrambled in behind a low rock formation about a dozen yards from the canyon exit, everyone else was in place. Peering out from behind their cover with his Winchester gripped in both hands, O'Brien noted that just about every sign of

177

their presence had been wiped out. Good. His eyes drifted to the left, and he saw a couple of Angel's men hunkered behind a rockfall piled against the base of the canyon's western wall; then right, to see two more in similar positions of readiness. The rest of the men, he knew, were scattered behind cover at the far end of the ravine, ready to close the trap as soon as the unsuspecting *federales* rode past them.

An expectant hush descended upon Blood Canyon. A minute passed. Ten minutes passed. Fifteen minutes later they heard the distant creak and jingle of the *federales* entering the canyon by way of its farthest end.

Crouching there in the super-hot noon heat, O'Brien felt a tingle of anticipation wash across his skin. Quickly he blotted his palms on the legs of his pants, then exchanged a brief, serious glance with Angel.

The sounds were growing steadily in volume now, and he, like Angel, chanced a look around the warm grey boulder, not over it, to check on the progress of the Government troops.

At first the trail ahead seemed empty. Then, just visible through the heat-haze, he made out a movement, and tensed. He saw them clearly now, in their chocolate-coloured charro sombreros and olive-green uniforms. Judging from the way they slumped in their saddles, they were dog-tired. There were, as Grady had estimated, about fifteen of them, under the command of a twenty-five-year-old captain, who rode at their head. Each man wore a sidearm, and a standard issue Marlin rifle slung across his back.

Yellow sunlight flashed briefly on the bugle carried by the second man in line. He, like the rest of them, wore a buff-coloured shirt beneath his olive-green vest. Behind him came the others, riding two abreast. Three ranks in, two of the *soldados* trailed heavy-laden pack-mules. If O'Brien hadn't known of the wealth those canvas-wrapped bundles held, he might have assumed they carried supplies and nothing more. Flanking the pack-animals rode two more troopers, red-faced, hot as hell, careless in their vigilance.

Finally, behind the mules came another three ranks of soldiers, riding two abreast. The entire column was strung out loosely within the confines of the canyon. The steady clatter-jingle of their passage echoed back from the ravine's walls.

O'Brien felt a bead of sweat trickle slowly down his left cheek. The muscles in his arms tensed even further. The captain was now perhaps eighty feet from their position.

To O'Brien's left, Angel slowly raised his Henry repeater and drew a bead on the officer. Ten seconds ticked by. Then, almost imperceptibly, Angel's finger tightened on the trigger.

His shot tore the air apart and exploded loose sand about six feet in front of the captain's high-stepping bay. For a moment there was shock on the faces of the men in the column. Then came confusion. The officer's horse side-stepped and pranced skittishly. Behind him, his men struggled to control their own spooked mounts and unlimber their guns.

Then Angel came out from behind the boulder with a fresh shell under the Henry's hammer and the barrel aimed directly at the captain's chest. 'Stay exactly as you are, all of you!' he yelled above the panicky din. 'There's no need for anyone to die so long as you do as I say!'

As if to reinforce his words, the rest of his men, O'Brien included, appeared from their hiding-places to menace the *federales* still further with handguns and rifles.

The troopers' surprise was almost pathetic. They had assumed themselves to be completely alone in the canyon. Never before had they encountered trouble on these secret trips they ran for the Minister of Finance, but now it looked as if complacency had been their downfall.

It could still go either way, though. They could surrender and have done with it, or they could fight.

And their captain decided to fight.

With a cry of *'Maldecir!'* he tore a Lefauchex pistol from his belt and triggered the shot that started the battle proper.

Suddenly the canyon was trembling to the sound of gunfire. Men yelled and horses screamed. Angel fired his Henry again and the *federale* captain flipped backwards off his horse to land stone-cold dead with a bullet in his chest.

Retaliation was swift, however. The bugler, bringing his Marlin around with surprising speed, returned fire and shot Angel up somewhere high; O'Brien didn't see exactly where, he was too busy putting the sonofabitch out of action before he could cause any more damage.

A horse fell, spilling its rider. One of Angel's men – Luis – hunched up under the impact of no fewer than three slugs, then fell to the sand. Another *federale* left his saddle, clutching a gore-stained chest; one more tumbled sideways, spraying his companion with a mixture of brain and skull-bone.

One of the pack-mules wheezed and went down splay-legged. Another of Angel's men staggered and fell behind a patch of prickly pear, wounded but not dead. The noise was deafening; a constant rattle of gunfire, the high nervous screeching of terrified or wounded horses, the sounds of men yelling in pain or defiance – and the blood-red walls of *Cañon de Sangre* amplifying all of it...

His nerve snapping, one of the Government troopers suddenly jammed his heels into his horse and started for the canyon exit at a gallop. His handgun was out and he was firing at everyone and everything, including his own comrades. In his panic he shot one of them in the chest, then tore a red chunk out of the canyon wall with another indiscriminate shot.

O'Brien, spotting him thundering ever closer, hurried over to Angel. The revolutionary had fallen onto his back and his face was slick with blood. Incredibly, however, he was still alive and conscious, though dazed. Tossing his Winchester aside, O'Brien grabbed him under the arms and dragged him to the safety of the rocks just as the frightened trooper surged past.

Twisting around, O'Brien watched him speed by, knowing that he couldn't allow him to get away. When this was all over, Angel and the survivors of his band would need time to get away before the alarm was raised; time they wouldn't get if that coward managed to summon reinforcements. So he drew his Colt, snap-aimed and fired – and blew the fleeing trooper into the hereafter.

A scream drew his attention. His head snapped around just as Grady went down under the hooves of a Government horse. The big-bellied American was lost beneath a screen of dust for a moment. Then his screaming stopped.

O'Brien came out from behind the rocks, feeling his fury rising fast. Four days earlier, he'd have considered all the Angel's men as enemies. Now, though, they were his brothers in blood. And by God, he was going to avenge the ones who fell.

Snatching his Winchester up in his left hand, he used both long gun and Colt to drill the *federale* aboard the flailing horse in the guts. As the trooper crashed to the ground, spraying claret, O'Brien moved deeper into the fray.

A riderless horse bore down on him. He

dodged to one side to avoid it. A *federale* on foot came at him with a bayonet held high. He shot the soldier in the head and moved on.

Time loses all meaning to men in battle. So it was with O'Brien. He had no grasp of seconds, minutes or hours. All he knew was the awful noise of conflict, of stepping over the bodies of men and horses, of firing the Colt and the Winchester until both clicked on empty, and curling his lip at the coppery stench of blood rising up from out of the red-stained sand.

Gradually, however, some part of his mind still conscious of such things, told him that the roar of gunfire was growing more sporadic; that even the cries of the wounded and dying were becoming intermittent.

Pretty soon there'd be no-one left to kill.

And that's just the way it turned out.

Before much longer, silence descended upon Blood Canyon. Bodies were scattered along virtually its entire length. The only men still standing were Angel's – all but three, who had died during the fight.

Reloading his Colt, O'Brien steadied himself against the wave of exhaustion he knew would claim him at any moment. It was always the same, once the action was over. That's when you realized how much all the killing had taken out of you.

Around him, Angel's men began to check on the dead, remove the peso-laden packs from the dead mule, patch their wounds. O'Brien shoved the Colt back into leather and watched Maria appear at the far end of the canyon. She ran towards the rocks behind which he'd left Angel, and he followed.

By the time he got there, Maria was cradling her lover's head in her lap. Angel looked ghastly. Those patches of his face not stained by the blood from his head-wound looked as pale as paper. He had also thrown up over his shirt.

Setting down his Winchester, O'Brien knelt beside the revolutionary. Using his neckerchief, he gently dabbed blood away from Angel's forehead.

After a while Maria cleared her throat and asked, 'O'Brien … will he … is he…?' He looked up at her. She didn't really want to voice the question, because she didn't really want to hear the answer.

But he had good news for her. 'The bullet only gashed him,' he reported. 'Here, see? Looks worse than it is. But he'll have a sore head for a week or so. Might be as much as a month before he'll feel like moving around under his own steam. But he'll live, Maria. Do you hear me? He'll *live*.'

Tears welled up in her hazel eyes and her small frame was racked by a mixture of sobs and chuckles. 'Oh ... oh, thank God ... thank G-God...'

As emotion choked off the rest of her words, O'Brien nodded dumbly. He could only agree – *thank God*.

As men die, so that day died. But by the time the sun finally disappeared beyond the horizon, leaving the dark sky lit only by distant, flickering stars, the Angel's depleted band were camped in the low, verdant hills many miles to the west.

Now, with guards posted and a meal of jack-rabbit stew behind them, the survivors smoked cigarettes and drank coffee, quiet in recollection of their fallen comrades.

Angel lay stretched out on a blanket among some thick, springy bunch-grass not far from the small fire. Maria had cleaned him up while the others had rigged a travois and made ready to quit Blood Canyon. For the rest of the afternoon, the revolutionary had dozed fitfully. Sometime around five o'clock, however, he'd woken up, summoned a smile for Maria, a few weak words of congratulation for his men and a soft, sad farewell to their dead. He'd been awake, but resting, ever since.

O'Brien stood some little way off from the others, savouring the bitterness of the coffee as he listened to the small sounds nocturnal animals made coming to drink at the clear pool not so far away. The hills surrounding them were gentle and rolling, spattered with clusters of yellow-flowered wedelia and tagetes. It was a beautiful location, a lifetime away from the horrors of Blood Canyon.

Tomorrow Angel's band would be heading further west to lick their wounds and figure out how best to distribute the money they'd stolen. But for O'Brien it was the end of the trail, at least as far as the revolution was concerned.

'We'll miss you, *mi amigo*,' Angel had husked once O'Brien had announced his intentions over supper. 'Maria here tells me you were a demon during that fight back at the canyon.'

A self-conscious smile twitched at O'Brien's lips. 'And I'll miss riding with you,' he confessed. *'All* of you.'

But, as he said, he had other business to finish, in Tanapa, Del Rio and finally,

Crystal City; and although he was sick of killing, he couldn't wait to deal with the fighting still to come.

NINE

One hundred and fifty kilometers – the distance between Frontera and Tanapa – is approximately ninety miles. In their haste to see the prisoner they believed to be held in Tanapa, Colonel Redarte and Captain Gerardo completed the journey in just under two days.

But almost as soon as they urged their lathered mounts onto the small, sleepy town's main street, both officers became aware that something about the place was not quite *right*.

The time was a little before six o'clock, and already the setting sun had dyed the sky, the land and the low, off-white adobes clustered there in that semi-arid basin a breathtaking scarlet. From the stable on their right came the regular clang of a blacksmith's hammer. In the small, whitewashed church at the end of the street, they heard a mixed congregation singing a hymn. A group of children were playing in the dirt on main street, but rather than direct their horses around them, both Redarte and Gerardo kept them trotting straight ahead, so that the children finally had to scamper away or stay and get stomped.

It was probably in that moment that the *colorados* realized exactly what was wrong. It was *fear*. The children had shown them the fear and grudging respect they had learned to enjoy. But the *peones* they had passed on their way in, be they male or female, elderly or in the prime of life – none of them had displayed that air of subservience which had been so apparent in Frontera.

Neither the colonel nor the captain commented on this curious lack of deference, but both of them remained acutely, and *uncomfortably*, aware of it as they reined in before the small *calabozo*.

Dismounting and flipping their reins across the hitch-rack in front of the jailhouse, the two officers brushed trail-dust from their sleeves and tugged their tunics into smarter, more precise lines. The worst of the day's heat was behind them now, and it looked as if the evening was going to be fine and pleasantly cool.

Glancing around, the *colorados* saw a few peasants in the baggy white clothes of the masses gathering on the opposite boardwalk to watch them. Under normal circumstances, such *peones* would run and hide from the authorities, such was the fear that *El Presidente*'s elite inspired within them.

This rabble, however, just stood there in the slowly lowering light, watching them.

Gerardo stepped up to the jailhouse door and turned the handle. The door refused to open. Frowning, he put his shoulder to it. No, it was closed firm.

'What is the matter?' asked Redarte as his assistant moved along the boardwalk to peer through the dusty glass of the window to the left of the door.

'There…' Gerardo paused, then shook his head. 'No, the place is locked up, and empty.'

'Empty?'

'*Si*. Maybe the local constable has gone home for the night.'

Redarte, annoyed by this, turned and stabbed his riding-crop at one of the men in the small group on the opposite boardwalk. 'Hi, you there!'

The man, a tall, heavily-boned *peon* with broad shoulders and straight black hair, stepped forward. He had a drooping moustache and gaps in his yellow teeth. 'Who, *me*?' he asked insolently.

'Yes, *you!*' Redarte snapped. 'Come here.

At once!'

The fellow did as he was told, but at a leisurely pace that spoke of impertinence. Redarte watched him come with colour rushing to his cheeks. Over in the church the singing stopped, and a few moments later the congregation began to file out.

At last the *peon* Redarte had summoned stood in the street before him, with his hands clasped behind his back. '*Si, senores?*' he asked casually.

Gerardo said, 'The constable, this Xavier Gonzalez. Where is he?'

'Constable, *senor?*'

'He's not in his office,' Gerardo explained sharply. 'Where is he? At home? Where does he live?'

The *peon* brought his left hand up to scratch thoughtfully at his moustache. 'Constable?' he repeated, exaggerating the word. 'Gonzalez, you say? There is no-one of that name in Tanapa, *senores*. We had a Gonzalez here once,' he said as an afterthought, just before his eyes iced over. 'But a year ago the *colorados* came and shot him.'

Redarte felt a sudden chill inside his stomach. He wasn't used to the feeling, and it took him a second or two to realize what it was; a sense of foreboding.

He glanced across at the church. The local *padre*'s flock numbered perhaps thirty *peones*. And all of them were slowly shuffling this way.

Meanwhile, Gerardo's frown had deepened. 'You mean you haven't got a constable named Gonzalez?' he demanded.

'I mean we haven't got a constable, *punto*,' the *peon* said with relish.

Gerardo looked dumbstruck. 'Then ... then what about this wire?' he asked, taking out the telegram the colonel had received from Frontera. 'The prisoner, O'Brien?'

At last a look of understanding came into the *peon*'s eyes as he brought his right hand out from behind his back, clutching a .45 Colt. 'Ah, O'Brien,' he said with a grim smile as his fellow townsfolk began to form a human ring around the two officers. '*Si. Senor* O'Brien will be along directly, *senores*. And from all I have heard, he is greatly looking forward to meeting you...'

They struggled, of course, for it was not in the nature of either man to go down without a fight. Redarte raised his riding-crop and struck one of the advancing *peones* in the face at the same time that Gerardo tried to pull his own gun from leather.

But there were too many of the peasants, and pretty soon the officers were over-powered, held firm and stripped of their weapons.

The big fellow with the .45 Colt produced a key and unlocked the jailhouse. The two *colorados* were thrown inside and the door was secured behind them. The room was small, stuffy and empty of furniture. Dust had settled everywhere. Although there were bars at the windows, there was no cell, and no cell-block. The need to house prisoners was probably rare in such a small, isolated town, and when it *did* arise, such detainees were doubtless chained to the dead oak-tree at the centre of the plaza.

Redarte and Gerardo pressed close to the windows of their prison, apprehensive, concerned about their fate and angry at the audacity of the working class. They watched the peasants split up and each go their separate ways. Pretty soon the street was empty, and not long after that the sky turned purple and visibility grew poor.

The *colorados* chose spots on the floor and sat down. Forcing themselves to remain calm, they tried to make sense of all that had happened. Then they tried to find some way of escaping their confinement.

Ten minutes later they sank back onto their haunches, frustrated in their attempts by thick adobe walls, barred windows and a hard-packed dirt floor it would take a week to tunnel through – not that they'd been left with anything they might use as a shovel, of course.

Somehow they got through the cold, silent, lonely night. The following morning the door was opened and while the big fellow with the .45 Colt kept them covered, a woman gave them each a cup of water and a chunk of stale black bread.

Redarte promised the pair of them great wealth if they would only allow the captain and himself to go free. He promised them riches, clemency, position, anything and everything that came to mind. But the man and the woman only ignored him.

The cups were taken back, the door was closed and locked, and the *colorados* were left alone again.

Supper came at six o'clock, by which time the two officers were in bad need of a wash and shave. Once again they tried to bribe their jailor. Once again the attempt was met with stony silence. After their meal – a watery bowl of vegetable stew each – their cups and cutlery were taken away.

The second night passed slowly. Mid-morning the next day, however, they were drawn to the dusty windows by the sounds of a commotion out in the street.

There was definitely a sense of expectancy in the muggy air. The townsfolk were beginning to gather in small knots along both sides of the street.

A moment later, the *colorados* realized why.

Although they'd never seen him before, they both recognized the man who rode in on the feisty little quarter-horse at once. Tall, compact, with a rugged face, close-cut salt-and-pepper hair and blue eyes showing clear beneath the brim of his tobacco-brown Stetson, this was without doubt the *hombre* they'd been hoping to arrest.

O'Brien.

As the *gringo* fighting-man reined in and dismounted, their jailor stepped out from the crowd to greet him. The two of them shook hands. Their jailor was all smiles, but O'Brien was serious, casting brief but constant glances toward the jailhouse.

It appeared that the Mexican was offering O'Brien some food or wine. O'Brien shook his head and said no. Then he pointed to the jailhouse and the Mexican nodded quickly. O'Brien held out one hand. The jailhouse key was placed into his palm. After that O'Brien excused himself and strode slowly up to the squat adobe building.

Inside, Redarte and Gerardo stepped back from the window and exchanged looks of disquiet. They heard O'Brien's bootfalls on the boardwalk, then the sounds he made fitting the key into the lock. Finally the door swung open with a dry creak and the *norteamericano* stood there looking at them.

He appeared younger than Redarte had expected, but only at first glance. When he peered closer, the colonel saw all the living that had been etched into the other man's face, and repressed a shudder.

A full minute ticked by. Then O'Brien said, 'You'd be Redarte.' His eyes travelled across the room to settle on the captain, and he smiled a smile that had no humanity in it at all. 'And you'd be Gerardo.'

Gerardo opened his mouth to speak, but Redarte interrupted him. 'Who are you?' he asked, feigning ignorance. 'Why have we been kept locked up like this?'

O'Brien's smile died without warning. 'Why?' he echoed. 'I'll tell you why. Because of what you sorry sonsofbitches did to a feller named Shep Morgan.'

To their complete surprise, he unbuckled

his gunbelt and threw it behind him, out into the street. Then he came deeper into the small room and booted the door shut.

Gerardo said nervously, 'What ... that is...'

'I'll make a deal with you,' O'Brien said, addressing them both. 'You get past me, you go free.'

Redarte snorted. *'What?'* In his surprise, he actually laughed. 'Are you *loco?* Two against one? Just because of some slow-witted cowboy who–'

'Yeah,' O'Brien cut in with quiet fury. 'Just because of some slow-witted cowboy.'

Gerardo flicked a glance across at his superior, then said, 'And if we beat you, get past you...?'

'You go free. The pair of you. My word on it.'

Redarte said, 'Can't we ... can't we discuss this?'

O'Brien said, 'No.'

And that was how the fight began.

Outside, standing in a wide half-circle around the small jailhouse, practically all the citizens of Tanapa stood in silence as they listened to the sounds of combat coming from within.

Men formed the bulk of the audience, men of all ages, but women were there as well, those not nursing or keeping an eye on babies and children, who were thankfully oblivious to the violence.

A collective intake of breath went through the crowd as one of the combatants inside the jailhouse suddenly hit the door with a crash and a groan. Every so often a figure could be glimpsed blurring past the windows, but it was hard to tell its identity. The crowd just had to content itself with the small, hard-slapping sounds of traded punches, the heavier thud of connecting kicks and the cries of men who were taking and receiving punishment almost too terrible to imagine.

At last it went very quiet inside the building. Nothing moved at either of the dusty, blank windows.

The citizens of Tanapa stood waiting in silence.

A moment later the jailhouse door opened and a figure staggered out into the sunlight.

Captain Raul Gerardo leaned up against the frame, his chest heaving from his recent exertions. His right eye was swollen and smudged, his bottom lip was twice its normal size, and split. Blood stained his chin, the front of his tunic, his skinned knuckles, and the bruising along his jaw appeared dark and painful.

He fairly glared at his audience.

'*Bastardos!*' he spat triumphantly.

Then a hand appeared from out of the shadows behind him, grabbed him by the shoulder and dragged him back into the darkness. Gerardo's startled yelp was interrupted by the sudden, harsh crack of impacting fists. Then they all heard the *colorado* slump to the floor.

Thirty seconds passed before O'Brien came out of the jailhouse, beaten and bruised himself, but victorious, too. He stared into the faces of the crowd, but not one of them returned his look. They were silent, impassive, and their eyes were on the empty doorway behind him.

He reached up and wiped a dribble of blood off his jaw. He knew what was going through their minds. They were remembering the twelve young men the *colorados* had come and taken one night, and executed on suspicion of treason.

He looked at the local telegrapher, who had also doubled as the *colorados*' jailor. The man held a rope in his hands. So did the man beside him. The ends of both lengths of hemp had been fashioned into nooses.

'Did you kill them, *senor?*' asked the tele-grapher.

O'Brien shook his head. 'Punished them the way they punished my friend Morgan,' he husked. 'That was all.'

The telegrapher smiled unpleasantly. 'Good,' he said.

O'Brien sagged a little, tired as hell, and stepped down into the dirt. He knew what was coming next, and he wanted no part of it, so he jammed one foot into the stirrup of his comfortable old Texas double-rig and hauled himself back aboard the quarter-horse.

As he walked the animal back the way he'd come, the townsfolk started shuffling towards the jailhouse, their intentions all too plain.

He made it to the end of the street just as Redarte began to scream for mercy. Again and again he yelled, *'Compasion! Compasion!'* But the sadistic sonofabitch didn't realize that where the *colorados* were concerned, the ears of Tanapa were deaf.

Three nights later O'Brien rode into the Texas Ranger barracks at Del Rio and swung down outside the stable not far from the small, neat row of adobe dwellings intended for use by Rangers with dependents. Not so long before, one of those little houses had been a temporary home to the man who'd called himself the Angel's father. But now...?

It was just a little after seven o'clock. The sky was already turning the colour of dust, and for once the Ranger barracks appeared to be quiet and restful.

O'Brien had just handed his reins over to the duty stable-man when he heard a door click open in the administration block on the northern edge of the courtyard. He turned as an oblong wedge of yellow lamplight spilled out onto the sand. Then the tall, solid silhouette of Captain Daniel Taylor stepped into the frame to block it out.

'O'Brien?' he asked. 'O'Brien, is that you?'

O'Brien went over to him and took the other man's hand. They shook like old friends, although Taylor had been anything but cordial the day O'Brien had taken the Salazar job on. The Texas Ranger had not approved of men like O'Brien. He'd made that plain. But from the looks of it, maybe things had changed.

'Hello, Taylor,' O'Brien greeted him. 'You got my wire?'

'About Molina and his daughter? Sure.'
'And?'

'Quit fretting,' Taylor said, a rare smile touching his tanned visage, twisting his narrow lips up and bringing warmth to his cynical blue eyes. 'I arrested 'em straight away and sent word on to the capital.' His smile turned into a chuckle. 'You know, I don't mind telling you, the Governor was furious. Ordered me to ship 'em off to him *pronto.*'

A word O'Brien had heard more than once during the last fortnight suddenly sprang to mind. 'I guess nobody likes being manipulated,' he said mildly.

'You never spoke a truer word,' the captain agreed, running a splay-fingered hand through his black-but-greying hair. 'Now, come on in and take the weight off a spell. Lord, but it sounds like you've had some high old times the last coupla weeks.'

Taylor led him down a white-walled hallway and into his office. The place hadn't changed all that much from O'Brien's previous visit. There in the low, saffron-coloured light of the Rochester lamp he saw the desk, chairs, file cabinet and map of Texas he remembered so well from the day when all this had begun.

'Sit down, O'Brien,' Taylor urged. He went

around to his side of the desk, sat down, opened a drawer and took out two glasses and a bottle of Tennessee sipping-whiskey that was still two-thirds full. 'Now, let's hear all about it.'

'In a minute,' O'Brien replied, accepting the proffered glass with a nod of thanks. 'I've got a question first.'

'Ask it, then.'

'What'll happen to Molina and his daughter? When they reach the capital, I mean.'

Taylor sipped at the contents of his own glass and assumed a thoughtful frown. 'That's kind of difficult to say,' he answered slowly. 'But I don't suppose any of it will ever come to court. Relations between our two countries being strained even at best, nobody's going to want to make an international incident out of it.' He sat back. 'No; it's my guess that the Governor will chastise 'em good and proper, but in the end he'll just send 'em home with orders never to set foot on U.S. soil again.'

O'Brien nodded. 'That's about what I figured.' He was silent for a moment, until he brightened. 'Now, what were you saying?'

'I wanted to hear all about what happened to you down in Mexico,' Taylor replied. 'But before you start, I'd better give you this.'

From another drawer he took a small manilla envelope, which he tossed casually onto the desktop.

'What's that?' O'Brien asked.

'The money *"Señor Salazar"* promised to pay you for killing his son.'

O'Brien's surprise showed on his face, for he'd resigned himself to going the loser on that. 'He never gave you that *willingly*,' he said over the rim of his glass.

'No,' Taylor grinned, 'he didn't. He had other things on his mind as we were arresting him, so I kind of … *appropriated* it from his considerable funds before we packed him up and sent him on to Austin.' He sobered suddenly, and looked embarrassed. 'I figured you had that money coming,' he said quietly.

O'Brien reached out and picked up the envelope. Without bothering to check the contents, he slipped it into one of his wolf-skin jacket's inside pockets.

'Good health,' said Taylor.

O'Brien raised his glass. 'Long life.'

They drank.

Sometime after midnight O'Brien left the administration block and paused under the bright Texas stars, allowing the cool night breeze to chase away some of his whiskey-induced euphoria.

Before he could properly consider the Salazar affair to be over, he still had one last chore to tend. And at first light tomorrow – that was, *today* – he'd ride southeast to Crystal City and see to it.

For he was still beholden to Shep Morgan. He owed him for one kindness after another. More importantly than that, however, he also figured he owed the man an explanation for all the events into which he'd unwittingly become enmeshed.

And O'Brien was a man who always paid his debts.

As he ambled across to the dark blotch of shadow which marked the position of the stables, intending to bed down in a spare stall, he thought about the big, homely cowboy, who was shy around women. O'Brien never had bought him that drink he owed him. But feeling *'Senor* Salazar's' bloodmoney against his ribs, he figured to buy the big man a whole damn' saloon, if that's what it took to say thank you to a friend.

The publishers hope that this book has given you enjoyable reading. Large Print Books are especially designed to be as easy to see and hold as possible. If you wish a complete list of our books please ask at your local library or write directly to:

Dales Large Print Books
Magna House, Long Preston,
Skipton, North Yorkshire.
BD23 4ND

This Large Print Book, for people
who cannot read normal print,
is published under the auspices of

THE ULVERSCROFT FOUNDATION

... we hope you have enjoyed this book.
Please think for a moment about those
who have worse eyesight than you ...
and are unable to even read or enjoy
Large Print without great difficulty.

You can help them by sending a
donation, large or small, to:

**The Ulverscroft Foundation,
1, The Green, Bradgate Road,
Anstey, Leicestershire, LE7 7FU,
England.**
or request a copy of our brochure for
more details.

The Foundation will use all donations
to assist those people who are visually
impaired and need special attention
with medical research, diagnosis
and treatment.

Thank you very much for your help.